W9-CER-769

To the memory of my mother, Pauline Kengué.

To L. Vague, always so close, the other light . . .

—ALAIN MABANCKOU

WITHDRAWN
No longer the property of the
Boston Public Library.
Sale of this material benefits the Library

BLUE
WHITE
RED

GLOBAL AFRICAN VOICES
Dominic Thomas,
EDITOR

BLUE
WHITE
RED

A NOVEL

ALAIN MABANCKOU

TRANSLATED BY ALISON DUNDY

Indiana University Press   Bloomington and Indianapolis

This book is a publication of

Indiana University Press
601 North Morton Street
Bloomington, Indiana 47404-3797 USA

iupress.indiana.edu
Telephone orders   800-842-6796
Fax orders   812-855-7931

© 2013 by Indiana University Press
Original French edition © 1998 by Présence Africaine

All rights reserved
No part of this book may be reproduced or utilized in any form
or by any means, electronic or mechanical, including photocopying
and recording, or by any information storage and retrieval system,
without permission in writing from the publisher. The Association
of American University Presses' Resolution on Permissions
constitutes the only exception to this prohibition.

⊛ The paper used in this publication meets the
minimum requirements of the American National Standard
for Information Sciences—Permanence of Paper for Printed
Library Materials, ANSI Z39.48-1992.

Manufactured in the United States of America

Library of Congress Cataloging-in-Publication Data

Mabanckou, Alain, 1966– author.
    [Bleu, Blanc, Rouge. English]
    Blue White Red : A Novel / Alain Mabanckou ; translated by Alison Dundy.
        pages cm. — (Global African Voices)
    ISBN 978-0-253-00791-9 (pbk. : alk. paper) — ISBN 978-0-253-00794-0
    (e-book) 1. Africans—France—Fiction. I. Dundy, Alison, translator. II. Title.
    PQ3989.2.M217B5513   2013
    843.914—dc23
                                                    2012042988

1 2 3 4 5   18 17 16 15 14 13

CONTENTS

TRANSLATOR'S INTRODUCTION

ALAIN MABANCKOU'S writing is like a Chinese line drawing. His economy of words is a brushstroke that reveals a subject's inner and outward character and an aching longing for place. Moki is a village hero in *Blue White Red* because he becomes a "Parisian," the title conferred on those who "make it" in Paris. His presence there transforms a village father, who now holds forth in the proper *French French* of Guy de Maupassant, as befits a man whose son is in the country of *Digol*. Moki chastises his wannabes for speaking *in French* but not *French* and cautions those who dream of emulating his leap from the former colony to the métropole: *Paris is a big boy.* Not for kids.

In Alain Mabanckou's text, it is apparent when people break into French for affect to emphasize their class status and distance themselves from the miserable economic and political circumstances of postcolonial Africa. *French French* is generally italicized in the original novel. In an English translation of the book, I wrestled with how to convey the complex nesting of languages, French bursting out in conversations in African languages and vice versa, without flattening the contours of the text in English. I experimented with leaving the italicized French in French, followed by an English translation. That device, however, proved too heavy to carry over the course of the whole novel and drew attention to the translation instead of the originality of Alain Mabanckou's book.

I switched back to translating the *French French* into English, but left it in italics. This note is therefore to help readers understand that italicized text denotes not merely emphasis in spoken language but a shift to a different language for added emphasis. Some words remain in French to allow an English reader to travel with Alain Mabanckou to the places he writes about. That requires leaving home to wander *rues*, not streets, hop the Métro, not the subway, and calculate the kilometers, not miles, whizzing past as a captured *sans-papiers* is driven in defeat in the back of an unmarked police car to detention.

This book exists because of my enthusiasm for Alain Mabanckou's novel and because Susan Harris obtained permission to publish a short excerpt on the Words without Borders website. It also exists because Dee Mortensen at Indiana University Press persevered for years to secure the rights to bring out the full text. Many thanks to Dominic Thomas for his careful reading of the translation and his suggestions, which finally brought *Blue White Red* into print for English readers as part of the Global African Voices series.

Alison Dundy, January 2012

AFRICAN MIGRATION AND AFRICAN *DANDYS*

DOMINIC THOMAS

ALAIN MABANCKOU was born in 1966 in the city of Pointe-Noire in the Republic of Congo. After completing college in the Congo, he studied law in Paris and worked in the field of corporate law. Eventually he abandoned the legal profession and moved to the United States, where he is a professor of French and Francophone studies at the University of California, Los Angeles (UCLA).

Mabanckou has produced poetry, short stories, and several novels with such esteemed publishers as Gallimard, Présence Africaine, Le Serpent à Plumes, and Seuil. His novels include *Les Petits-Fils nègres de Vercingetorix* (2002), *African Psycho* (2003), *Verre cassé* (2005), *Mémoires de porc-épic* (2006), *Black Bazar* (2009), and *Demain j'aurai vingt ans* (2010), and he is the recipient of important awards, including the Prix Ouest-France Etonnants Voyageurs, Prix du Livre RFO, Prix des Cinq Continents de la Francophonie, and most notably the Prix Renaudot, one of France's most prestigious literary prizes. He is also the author of two works of nonfiction: *Lettre à Jimmy* (on American writer James Baldwin, 2007) and *Le sanglot de l'homme noir* (on contemporary race relations in France, literature, and African history, 2012). Mabanckou emerged as a spokesperson of sorts for the collective of writers who published the *Manifesto for a World Literature in French* in 2007, a thought-provoking declaration that has endeavored to bring greater attention to the global diversity of writing in French.

Mabanckou is widely considered one of the most influential
African writers at work today, and he was recently described in
a major article in the *Economist* as the "Prince of the Absurd."[1]
    Blue White Red was Mabanckou's first novel, published in
1998. He was awarded the Grand Prix Littéraire de l'Afrique
Noire, the jury having rightly recognized the emergence of
a genuinely new voice. Mabanckou's novel announced new
directions for the Francophone African novel, expanding upon
earlier themes of exile, migration, and travel, as he explored
the trials and tribulations that accompany those attempts at
living *between* Africa and France and *in* Africa in France.[2] In
turn, these new diasporic communities provide us with fasci-
nating insights on the nature of twenty-first-century global-
ized, postcolonial, transnational networks—those very themes
that are shaping the series Global African Voices at Indiana
University Press.
    In *Blue White Red*, the reader will discover those elements
that have become defining characteristics of Mabanckou's
œuvre: a combination of humor and linguistic innovation (the
inspiration can be traced to his esteemed compatriot Sony
Labou Tansi), alongside discerning commentary and analysis
of the contemporary challenges facing the African continent
and in particular African youth. The period following African
independence from colonial rule was devoted to the daunting
task of nation-building, and now that some fifty years have
elapsed since that process began, young people often find
themselves alienated, disenfranchised, and with limited professional opportunities. As such, they are compelled to seek
out employment prospects outside of their country of birth
and invariably move toward the relatively more prosperous
regions outside of the African continent. However, these devel-
opments in migration patterns have also coincided with the

---

1. "Prince of the Absurd: The Mad, Bad Fiction of Congo's Alain
Mabanckou," *Economist,* July 7, 2011.
    2. Dominic Thomas, *Black France: Colonialism, Immigration, and
Transnationalism* (Bloomington: Indiana University Press, 2007).

shifting framework of twenty-first-century economic, social, and political realities, which have yielded increasing control and legislation. Migrants now find themselves in additionally precarious circumstances, forced to confront racial profiling and arbitrary police round-ups and avoid detention centers and deportation procedures. In this framework, migratory "push" and "pull" pressures remain very real, yet the centrifugal draw of Paris has survived the end of colonialism.

In *Blue White Red*, Mabanckou tackles interesting facets of migration, bringing together two migrant groups, namely, the Peasants and the Parisians. The Peasants are economic migrants who have elected to leave the African continent in order to seek employment in Europe. The Parisians, however, are represented by a very particular category made up of African *Dandys*, whose members are mostly young men lured to France by the desire to acquire designer clothes in order to enact the all-important *descent* on the homeland and display their new acquisitions. The practice, known as *La Sape*, has roots in colonial times given that the attempt at controlling the colonized body through a standardization of clothing was challenged by the refusal to partially assume the external appearance of the other.[3] *La Sape*, whose practitioners are known as *sapeurs*, designates the Society for Ambiencers and Persons of Elegance (some of its more famous adherents include the musicians Koffi Olomide and Papa Wemba). As Didier Gondola explains, with growing urbanization, "fashion, for instance, was one of the elements that manifested this gap [gender gap] and fostered the invisibility of women and, by contrast, the visibility of men."[4] Analogous mechanisms of social control were to be found in postcolonial Africa. Shortly

3. See Phyllis M. Martin, *Leisure and Society in Colonial Brazzaville* (New York: Cambridge University Press, 1995).
4. Didier Gondola, "Popular Music, Urban Society, and Changing Gender Relations in Kinshasa, Zaire (1950–1990)," in *Gendered Encounters: Challenging Cultural Boundaries and Social Hierarchies in Africa*, ed. Maria Grosz-Ngaté and Omari H. Kokole (New York: Routledge, 1997), 70.

after his election in 1970, Congo-Zaire's President Mobutu outlined his project of "zaïrianisation," effectively deploying a campaign of "authenticity" whose guidelines were provided by a conscious distancing from European influences, including when it came to clothing. People were encouraged to wear the short-sleeved "abacost" suit (which literally means "down with the suit," or *à bas le costume* in French). *La Sape* is thus a strategy of resistance and self-affirmation, "there to conceal his social failure and to transform it into apparent victory,"[5] and as Achille Mbembe has shown, "In the postcolony, magnificence and the desire to shine are not the prerogative only of those who command. The people also want to be 'honored,' to 'shine,' and to take part in celebrations . . . in their desire for a certain majesty, the masses join in the madness and clothe themselves in cheap imitations of power to reproduce its epistemology."[6]

Blue White Red thus examines the tenuous relationship between Parisians and Peasants as they endeavor to share space in Paris's diasporic African communities, while also maintaining their distance from one another. Their objectives are, of course, quite different. The novel offers an insider's glimpse at the topography of "African Paris," with its produce markets, hair salons, music stores, and so on, but the focus is provided by the survival skills, resourcefulness, and tricks performed by the *sapeurs,* who circulate "at the margins of the law."[7] As Lydie Moudileno has argued, "The peasant represents a threat to the fiction of emigration,"[8] and *Blue White Red* "exposes not only the actions and the discourse that perpetu-

---

5. Didier Gondola, "Dream and Drama: The Search for Elegance among Congolese Youth," *African Studies Review* 42, no. 1 (April 1999): 31.

6. Achille Mbembe, *On the Postcolony* (Berkeley: University of California Press, 2001), 131–33.

7. See Janet MacGaffey and Rémy Bazenguissa-Ganga, *Congo-Paris: Transnational Traders on the Margins of the Law* (Bloomington: Indiana University Press, 2000).

8. Lydie Moudileno, *Parades postcoloniales: La fabrication des identités dans le roman congolais* (Paris: Karthala, 2006), 124.

ates the Parisian myth, but also points to the complicity of the migrants when it comes to certain elements of their experience."[9] Indeed, this could be considered the central purpose of the novel. Yet, paradoxically, this also happens to be where Mabanckou's creative genius shines through, as he brings to life the originality and vibrancy of the *sapeurs.*

Blue White Red offers hilarious descriptions of the *sapeurs'* gatherings. The playfulness reverberates in the language, so brilliantly captured in Alison Dundy's translation, which is as seamless as the meticulously choreographed performances Mabanckou stages. Appropriating clothes made by a plethora of international designers such as J.-M. Weston, Valentino, Gianni-Versace, and Yves Saint-Laurent, the *sapeurs*, writes Justin-Daniel Gandoulou, now "initiate the dance of designer labels, which consists in allowing the protagonists to dance and show off their clothes and designer labels."[10] Often having altered the color of their complexion, deliberately gained weight (to be portly implies opulence!), and endeavored to express themselves in only the very best "French from France" (even committing to memory poems and passages from canonical French authors), they are ready to begin the "battle" for bragging rights:

> My adversary stunned me by executing an acrobatic leap that left the spectators cheering hysterically. He was dressed in a black leather outfit with boots and a black buckskin helmet. He smoked a fat cigar and turned his back on me—one way to ignore me and make a fool of me. I moved calmly toward the center of the dance floor. I was wearing a colonial helmet and a long cassock that swept the ground when I moved. I held a Bible in my right hand, and while my adversary had his back turned to me, I read aloud in an intelligible voice a passage from the Apocalypse of Saint John. The audience was euphoric, swept away by my originality.

9. Ibid., 128–29.
10. Justin-Daniel Gandoulou, *Au cœur de la sape: Mœurs et aventures de Congolais à Paris* (Paris: L'Harmattan, 1989), 209.

In *Blue White Red*, the paradigmatic figure all young men seek to emulate is Moki. Recognized as an accomplished *sapeur*, his status in the African community is enhanced with each *descent* on the Congo. As Didier Gondola notes, "The expression *milikiste* designates the young Congolese who live in Europe and, to a lesser extent, in North America. . . . *Miliki* in Lingala is the plural for *mokili*, the 'world,' and has become synonymous for Europe. When the French suffix is added, the word identifies the young who made it to Europe."[11] Whether eager "to define their social distinctiveness"[12] through fashion or to pursue economic opportunities elsewhere, the Peasants and Parisians share in the "blue-white-red dream" (an obvious allusion to the colors of the French flag), and as Mabanckou writes, "We were allowed to dream. It didn't cost anything. No exit visa was necessary, no passport, no airline ticket."

Ultimately, we are left pondering how to reconcile the multiple components and facets of the migration adventure—the hopes and aspirations of those that are left behind, the quotidian difficulties confronting the migrants, and the disappointment and shame that will accompany a failed migration to the North. . . . To this end, *Blue White Red* joins a distinguished library of African works, as Mabanckou narrates the latest chapter in the African French experience. This intertextuality is powerfully evident, as we are reminded of the father's parting words to his son, Laye, in Camara Laye's 1954 novel, *L'Enfant noir* (The Dark Child): "I knew quite well that eventually you would leave us."[13] In *Blue White Red*, Massala-Massala now listens to his own father's advice: "I have always thought that you would leave one day. Far, far away from here." Mabanckou's pioneering novel is thus concerned with the circulation of people but also of literature, and as such it raises important questions about African writing today, the places in which it is produced, published, and ultimately *read*.

11. Gondola, "Dream and Drama," 28.
12. Martin, *Leisure and Society*, 171.
13. Camara Laye, *L'Enfant noir* (Paris: Plon, 1954); *The Dark Child*, trans. James Kirkup (London: Collins, 1955), 181.

BLUE
WHITE
RED

The imagination culls its ingredients from reality.

Such is the price one has to pay to achieve a likeness. In the last resort, however, it is the author that must give his characters the fate he thinks is custom-fit to them, depending on the circumstances. From the time they are shaped, these characters borrow our ways. The good and/or the bad. None of the heroes (or antiheroes) presented here belong to any world other than the imagination.

OPENING

I'LL MANAGE TO GET MYSELF OUT OF THIS.

I don't know which side the sun rises from or sets anymore. Who will hear my complaints? I've completely lost my bearings here. My universe is limited to this isolation I've grown accustomed to. Could I have behaved differently? I ended up building a space deep in my heart that isn't enough for me. I follow deserted paths. I pass through ghost towns. I hear my footsteps on dead leaves. I startle the night birds sleeping on one leg. I stop. I start up the path again until the first glint of dawn . . .

Hold on to hope for as long as possible. Say, after all, nothing is lost in advance. I don't undress. It feels like this all unfolded in a single day, in a single night. A long day. A long night. I'm split between a pressing anxiety that fills my lungs and this false serenity dictated by the way the situation developed. I forgot to be who I had always been. Calm. Serene. Attentive. Who, in similar circumstances, would lift faithfulness above and beyond reality? Vanquished by fatigue, my back up against the wall, it's difficult for me to understand that I've come to that fateful moment, the one those in our small world dread, when the race ends in a cul-de-sac . . .

Believe me, it's not so much the confrontation that makes me hopeless; I broke with that. Instead, it's what I can foresee from here: all those wide-open eyes, all those hands held out, waiting for me. It's a promise each of us carries like a turtle carries its shell. I can't allow myself not to look at things from that angle. I can't suddenly ignore all that. They are waiting for me. I am their only hope. I feel entrusted with a mission that must be accomplished at all costs. Otherwise, what will I say to them? That I couldn't stick it out to the end? Will they forgive me? Will they understand me?

Things are going to happen really fast.

An almost logical continuation. I have never been a fatalistic preacher. I have always fought obstacles, even the most insurmountable. At some point, strength abandons us to our fate, as if to reassure itself that we can move beyond ourselves, without groaning, without wiping our brows, and without making the slightest grimace as evidence of our weakness. Then one feels alone. The wind howls above the rooftops. Little by little, the sun is eclipsed and leaves a lasting, scorching heat. The horizon unfolds, while the land, scattered with rough spots, leaves us no choice but a painful march and burning feet.

—m—

At bottom, I feel like I've anted up my fate and it will be decided by how the poker game is played. Some will think that I'm looking to justify myself, to plead atonement before the Supreme Being. I am far from thinking that. I'm not one to whimper over my fate or lie on the sly when the time comes to explain myself, even if that particular moment is the most painful for someone who has lived in our milieu, a world one doesn't escape from again once the door is shut.

Yes, the door that slams shut.

That mechanical noise, here, there. The clicking of the lock. Advancing footsteps. A hand gestures, pointing a finger at you, singling you out. And you, you say that you're in here for no reason. You raise your right hand. As high as possible. You swear. In the name of God. In the name of your family. They insist, they prove the opposite. Proof with supporting evidence. You were there, at that place, at that hour, with Mr. So-and-so, this is what you did, you left on this street, you passed a thin, small man in a suit. The man gave you an envelope, you took it, you opened it, you exchanged a few words, you got on the subway together. That's it. Would you like us to continue the description? Here's a photo. Take a good look. You're with the man in a suit. What do you have to say about it?

They've won.

I would like for everything to be put back in chronological order. For every link of the broken chain to be put back in its place. For every fact and every gesture to be faithfully repeated. To stop this confusion in my head. It's imperative for me to suppress this bad habit of rapidly reacting on impulse in the face of events, without taking the time to reflect maturely. That way, I would see more clearly and maybe clear a path out of here, even if my chances are, to put it mildly, pathetic.

I've stepped back a bit now that I'm heading, for better or worse, back to square one. And this path is not one of the easiest. To retrace one's footsteps is to confront the specter of one's past. I am not so intrepid. I'm worn out. I don't dare take a look at myself. It looks to me like I've lost weight, prominent jaw, hollow cheeks, dry lips, like the last time when, a few days before the two men arrived, I stared at myself in a basin of water in the middle of that courtyard in Seine-Saint-Denis under the watchful eye of the guard who ordered me to come back inside quickly. I pretended not to hear his barking. I dawdled, not convinced that the reflection in the basin was my own. I turned around, imagining that someone else was looking at his reflection over my shoulder. Those were the only occasions when I could take the time to make out my face. Otherwise, I was limited to guessing what it looked like when I lightly passed a hand under my chin to feel the roughness of my unkempt beard.

To this day, if I were to show anyone the first photo of me in Paris, tacked on the wall long ago in our room on rue du Moulin-Vert in the fourteenth arrondissement, they would be so shocked that it would almost cause a commotion.

It had been an exhausting, terrible forced march to get all the way here. It wasn't my feet that carried me but the unfolding

wave of events, and I realize from one day to the next that
my suffering isn't over, that once again I have to expect more
trouble ahead.

I had shown from the beginning that I possessed an immense
capacity to adapt. I had never outdone myself like that before.
Above all, I showed that I was capable of liquidating myself
into a milieu while adding my own personal touch, which
could prove decisive. And I could also work in collaboration,
as I did with Préfet later on. That I could dedicate myself to
the other members of the milieu, notably by assuring them
copious meals that they won't soon forget, except for ill will
on their part—and that would hardly surprise me.

This was a miscalculation, openly trashed by the entire
milieu after my grace period expired. It seemed that these
deeds were nothing but a drop of water in the ocean and that
I would need more enthusiasm if I wanted to see the end of
the tunnel someday.

Under these circumstances, one will understand that
silence, observation, and sometimes contempt lived inside me.
I thought that things would go in my favor, suturing the gap-
ing wounds here and there of my disillusionment. I saw the
distance sinking between my dirty past and the illusory cocoon
of a future.

I had no choice. I took the plunge.

—ɯ—

As soon as I look beyond my careless mistake, I can't see
anything except a cloud of dust. A plane takes off in a very low
sky during the dry season and lands at dawn the next day at
Roissy-Charles-de-Gaulle airport. It's as if I'd shut my eyes and
found myself all of a sudden on the other side of the gate. It
doesn't surprise me anymore that my first reaction was to vis-
cerally turn my back on all that. To deny reality and not take
the place that awaited me, or to be more precise, the position
I had been granted in this other universe.

To be sure, those of my ilk will treat me like a coward—a
débarqué, someone just off the boat—because I put up no resis-

tance whatsoever when I saw the two men coming toward me in that little deserted street.

The images come back to me, slightly blurry, one super-imposed upon another. Those pigeons that took flight and perched on the rooftops when they were disturbed. Me, too. I would also have liked to have been a dove. To have wings and lift myself above those buildings so I could survey how the situation developed. I was suddenly paralyzed by some sort of guilty conscience. A sense of malaise. It was as if I first had to pay a fine to recover the freedom to exist, to be myself. But this kind of liberty can't be bought. There's the weight of con-science, the embarrassment in front of this mirror that weighs the pros and cons of our actions.

I admit that I lack finesse, flair, and especially the scruples that made it possible for my companions to slip through the fine web of the net that awaited us. I don't know how they always managed to have nerves of steel, especially to evade the traps placed along our route at the opportune moments. In fact, they don't look at what's happening behind them because, as they say, run for your life—you don't have eyes in the back of your head. They adopt a blasé attitude and don't think about what's going to happen next; they act first. The rest doesn't concern them and will be resolved when the prob-lem is posed.

These are the basic precepts of our culture. Tested and proven elementary principles for all situations at all times. A dogma to cling to with your eyes shut. To use without hesi-tation at the right moment. I should have adopted that phi-losophy. If I wanted to achieve my goal, that's what I should have done. They made me understand that there was no other solution.

—m—

I put up no resistance when confronted by the two men. How could I pump my legs to run for my life when they were paralyzed and wouldn't hold me up anymore? Which direction would I have gone? I was rooted to the ground. Like a tree.

No, I put up no resistance whatsoever, and I have no regrets about that.

Escape? I fantasized about it.

I felt the time was coming. I couldn't foresee anything else happening. I certainly would have made the situation worse if I had done anything except give myself up. I wasn't totally wrong, since I saw this behavior again, a little later, in other circumstances, before other men supposedly charged with setting me straight. The result, however bitter, still seems acceptable to me today, with a few qualifications. Escape, frankly, would have changed things.

I stayed put.

I still can't get one question out of my head.

It had already occurred to me when I was in the car watching the scenery pass by, those mournful willows, those spindly fir trees, those trees, wind-whipped and shrunken by the cold of full-blown winter: why was it the same men who came back to arrest me in Seine-Saint-Denis eighteen months later and put me in the same white car, a Mazda, this time without the black chauffeur who had been so overzealous in Château-Rouge, that working-class neighborhood in the eighteenth arrondissement of Paris?

Indeed, they came eighteen months later.

They were waiting for that day. Or maybe they had been entrusted with the task to come back. They had to finish the job they themselves had started. I felt as if they had been assigned to track me from the beginning until the end.

They came. Both of them. Without the black guy.

They took me. Forced me into the Mazda. We drove all around the region. It seemed to me like we were turning around and around before picking up a boulevard on the perimeter (without letting anyone pass on our right), then the highway. We crisscrossed more regions than just Ile-de-France, but I wouldn't be able to name them today, even if I were asked under torture. As for the other regions, from the time I arrived in France, I had never been to any. What I do remember is that the car went at breakneck speed, really fast.

Some kind of race car with shot shock absorbers propelled us in fits and starts and lost its steering when the red needle on the speedometer clocked 160 kilometers per hour. The car spat blackish smoke every time the motor had a coughing fit. Nobody said a word. It seemed to me we had traveled a long way. A very long way. I would have guessed that we were traveling further from the region. The signs along the highway meant nothing to me at all. There was less housing, and it became more unusual with the passing of each kilometer marker, giving way to factories, to vast pastures without cattle, to rustic countryside under a thick fog that permitted nothing but ghostly shadows to appear. I guessed there was a plow here, haystacks over there, a combine, an old broken-down tractor in the distance, next to the highway; we were in backcountry.

But we kept on rolling.

After more than two hours on the road, we came to a silent place that, at first, I thought was a railway depot, because broken-down trains were parked all over the place. A mass grave for railway cars. I thought about elephants that go to cemeteries to protect themselves from prying eyes. Nuts and bolts and iron bars were strewn across the ground. Yellow safety helmets hung from the branches of the few trees in this spot. Railway workers' overalls hung from the windows of locomotives. It was quite a deserted site. Nobody around. Not the shadow of a life. We got out of the car, my arms still handcuffed to the big guy.

In the late morning, a dusting of white snow carpeted the ground and crunched under our feet. Mine were damp, frozen, and numb. I couldn't feel them anymore. I wasn't dressed for the weather. A blue cloth shirt over a black T-shirt. Jeans worn through at the knees, Spring Court sneakers on my feet. I shivered. The two men made great fun of this, decked out in military boots, heavy coats, lined gloves and hats that covered their ears as if they were crossing Siberia.

We had walked several hundred yards on foot. The engines and railway cars were far behind us. A vast expanse opened before us with a horizon of antiquated buildings. We hurried toward them. Crows punctured the fog, cavorting high in the sky, in search of the tallest ledge of those buildings, their wings clenched in the cold.

Four thugs pushed open the gate without batting an eye when we arrived. We crossed a large deserted courtyard marked by tracks of gigantic boots. This place had clearly been used before. I noticed a fenced soccer field on the other side, a few barbells, and just one basketball hoop. We headed straight for the tallest building and took the stairs that led to the basement. The two men dragged me down an interminable corridor. Our steps reverberated in rhythm, as if we had planned it. The silence gave the place the feeling of a decrepit penitentiary, abandoned if not outright haunted.

Awakened by the heavy silence of the place, I started to get worried. What had we come here to do? Did I deserve this isolation? Moreover, to be treated like this, was I a prisoner? That's what it looked like. I thought it unfair that they had taken me captive. I wasn't going to let them mistreat me this way. Certain things had to be clarified.

Many things.

First of all, I demand that you tell me why we're here. What did they say to you when you shoved me into the car? Answer me, sirs! Answer! Come on, give me an answer! Is this just for today? Until this evening? Until tomorrow? Or until the day after tomorrow?

Silence.

I wanted to express myself, explain, convince, tell them to give me a few minutes, just a few minutes. To ask a favor: take me back to rue du Moulin-Vert in the fourteenth arrondissement. Our building. The cars parallel-parked down the whole street. The Arab on the corner who let comrades buy on credit. The stairs. The window. The wool blankets. The plastic table. The camping stove on wheels. Which was the way to rue du Moulin-Vert?

They would drive me there. Maybe not.

They'd say, "What are you going to do back there? No, it's out of the question."

I would beg them again.

Nothing but this one last favor, please, sirs. They would no longer listen to me. Definitely wouldn't talk. Shut up! One more word and they'd have an excuse to beat me with a billy club. Follow them silently. Do what they want.

And wait.

—ᴍ—

The corridor became narrower the further we went. We went down several flights. The two men escorting me, one in front, the other behind, knew where to step. Their practiced, aloof attitude meant this was certainly routine. The bigger of the two must have been at least six feet tall. His primate arms hung down to his knees and he had to unshackle himself from me to be able to move with ease. The second man was not as tall. He turned around and looked me straight in the eye, a dark look of resolution. His thickset muscular bulk showed that he worked out assiduously.

We had been forced to walk lopsidedly and had to hunch over so we didn't bump into the stairs above our heads.

Finally, we got to a heavy iron door, equipped with no less than a dozen locks. One of the two men, the smaller one, took out a bunch of keys. He picked the wrong one several times. He muttered and cursed before finding the right one. The other one, without a word of warning, pushed me into the room. . . .

When the door slammed shut, it was as if night had fallen. I stayed still for a good minute with my eyes closed. I opened them gradually to accustom myself to the darkness. Then, little by little, a glint of light made its way through the barred holes of the building's air ducts, way above my head.

The silence would have been complete were it not occasionally punctured by quick footsteps, coughing, murmuring behind the door, and even sometimes, to my great surprise, by outbursts of resounding laughter that I heard coming from above this sort of cell.

So there was life in the building.

—∾—

Since then, I've been in this somber room, facing my shadow, which I see get up and walk without warning me. It comes and it goes. It gets up and sits down again, holding a hand to its cheek as if we formed just one entity and our fates were sealed forever.

All their warnings struck me as ridiculous. Even left outside, alone, I wouldn't find my way back. From the get-go, the idea of escaping never entered my head.

I repeat: I do not consider myself a prisoner. I have nothing to escape from. But them, would they believe me? Experience had proved the contrary to them. I have no doubt, people in my situation, incensed, tried anything and everything. Wait behind the door, pretend to fall into a complete faint, then grab the throat and don't let go of the man who would come toward them or bring in a meal.

If they sequestered me—I can't find a euphemism for the circumstance—in this sort of bunker, it's only to protect themselves against an eventual escape.

It is highly likely that a police van will come take us like damaged goods to put in storage before being disposed of later in a public dump, far away from everyday life. I say us because my intuition tells me that I'm not alone here.

Do I have neighbors of misfortune in the adjacent rooms? Nothing indicated I should think so. Or think not. If they are there, are they there for the exact same reason as me or at least a related one? Had we also been neighbors in Seine-Saint-Denis, or did they come from other places around Paris? No information at all. A complete wall. Night.

—∾—

The rank smell.

The room I was in had been unoccupied for a long time. In the dark, man's only reflex is to turn inward on himself. The dark reminds him that he is nothing but an infinitesimal speck without the blessing of the light of day. He can't set out to do anything, and he is reduced to groping his way.

I curled up in a corner across from the door. Fatigue tightened its grip on me. But don't sleep. Stay awake. Rub your eyelids. No, don't sleep. Don't do it, in order to see what is in store for me next. . . .

The dark plunged me into a hypnotic state.

It's impossible for me to separate dream from reality. Shadows walked in front of me. Faces. Places. Voices. I'm unable to associate this phantasmagoric universe with a specific situation. For me, all of this is still confused. I feel like I'm at the bottom of a cliff, slowly rising back up, deluded in the ascent by the prospect of false happiness, which I aim toward, flying through the sky. The wind gives me wings. I use them. All I've got to do is lift my arms to the sky to take flight. Is that why my eyelids grow heavy?

I stare at that smiling, reedy silhouette while I'm dozing off. I recognize the silhouette. I would recognize that one among thousands.

It's Moki.

It's him. Why does your face look a little thin to me? It's really you, Moki. I recognized you. And that man next to you? Who drove him all the way here? I recognize him, too. His name is Préfet. He's drunk. As usual. He's looking at his watch. As usual. He sizes me up, deciding that I'm the man for the job, that I'll do a good job with this business at the end of the month. I owe him that, I tell you, after everything he's done for me. You tell me it's also in my own self-interest; I should think about that, you add. Instead of staying put, not doing a damn thing, Préfet says. And you give him your agreement. I have nothing to say about that. My voice doesn't count. Préfet will come back to rue du Moulin-Vert the day after tomorrow. Very early in the morning. We'll make the rounds together. You made that decision together, a job for rookies, to use the words Préfet used that morning. Everyone has done this work. Even you, Moki, you assured me. Everybody started out with this. Later, I would do other things if I wanted to. It's a job that shouldn't be difficult for me to accomplish. You worked it out together—I know that, Moki. I'm talking to you. Why do you come after me even in my sleep? Do we remain connected even here? I make no mistake. It's definitely your face.

Where are you now? . . .

—ⱳ—

I would like for everything to be in chronological order. At times, memory seems like a mountain of garbage that has to be patiently sifted through just to retrieve a miniscule object, the trigger that sends everything adrift, linked together in a succession of events irrespective of a man's will.

The tangle of events burns my temples. I was surprised at how things happened. I would like for everything to be clear. That there be no ambiguity. I have nothing to hide. Not to mention nothing to lose. Much less, something to gain. I did not hurt anyone, as I will point out. I acted like all the others, those in our circle. I'm not one of those that holds back, and Moki knows that very well. Préfet is convinced of it, even though that guy is hard to please.

What's important at this point is to understand.

To look at everything without truncating or falsifying the facts. I don't want to relive the illusion that started me down this road. I figure I'll be accused of being a false friend, accused of treachery, or betrayal, and the height of irony, of ingratitude, me who has never been presumptuous and who gave the best of myself. That's what I expect.

It's difficult for me to step back from this. Things are happening fast. Tonight? Tomorrow? Day after tomorrow? I have no idea what day it is. My reminiscence is an unavoidable internal examination to ease my conscience, freed from the sludge of remorse that crushes my thoughts . . .

With perseverance and dogged determination for a shovel, I'll take whatever time it takes to exhume all those moments that catapulted me from near and far, all the way to this place, more than six thousand kilometers from the land where I was born.

PART ONE

The Country

It is better to dream one's life than to live it, though even living it is to dream it.

—Marcel Proust, *In Search of Lost Time*

IN THE BEGINNING, there was the name. A humdrum name. A two-syllable name: Moki . . .

At the beginning, there was that name.

Moki is standing in front of me. I see him again. He's talking to me. He is giving me instructions. He tells me to take care of the rest with Préfet. Don't ask him any questions. Just do what he asks me to do. Moki is there, his gaze turned upward toward the sky. He rarely takes a good look at his go-betweens. I listen to him. Continuously. Rapt.

Am I ready?

Have I seen to everything?

He is in a hurry. He doesn't have time. We have to hurry. *Don't sleep on your feet,* that's his expression. We're supposed to cross paths at noon at the Arc de Triomphe. Don't say a word to anyone. Come alone. Make sure that you're not being followed. Take a different route than the one we usually do. Don't get there too early. Waiting around is a bad sign. You'll end up getting caught that way. Be there on time. Not one minute later. Not one minute earlier. Everything happens so fast. You have to shape up. That's the way it is with Moki . . .

Moki is there.

I still don't realize that he's the one who made the arrangements to get me into France. I can't figure out that he's also the one who took me in and put a roof over my head in this country.

I was one of those who thought that France was for the others. France was for those who we used to call *the go-getters*. It was that faraway country, inaccessible despite its fireworks that shimmered even in the least of my dreams and that left me, when I awoke, with a taste of honey in my mouth. It is true, I had been secretly working in my field of dreams on the wish to cross the Rubicon, to go there someday. It was a common wish; there was nothing special about that wish. You could hear that wish expressed from every mouth. Who of my generation had not visited France *by mouth,* as we say back home. Just one word, *Paris,* was enough for us to meet as if by magic spell in front of the Eiffel Tower, at the Arc de Triomphe, and on the Champs Elysées. Boys my age seduced their girls, warming them with the serenade: *I'll be going to France soon. I'm going to live in the center of Paris.* We were allowed to dream. It didn't cost anything. No exit visa was necessary, no passport, no airline ticket. Think about it. Close your eyes. Sleep. Snore. And there we were, every night . . .

Reality caught up with us. The barriers stood insurmountably high. The first obstacle for me was my parents' poverty. We weren't dying of hunger, but a trip to France was nothing but a luxury to them. We could do without it. We could live without having gone there. Moreover, the Earth would continue to rotate. The sun would follow its course and would visit other faraway places; we would cross paths in the same places, in our fields or at the marketplace at slaughter time or when the peanuts were harvested. My parents would ruin themselves for no good reason by contributing to an adventure like that.

I imagined their response: "What the hell will you do in the white man's country? You abandoned your studies a long time ago!"

The other obstacle was my negative opinion of myself. I was hard on myself. I did not accord myself a single positive quality. I saw the dark side of things and imagined only the worst.

Convinced that I was a good-for-nothing, lacking self-motivation, I thought of myself as a sluggish, spineless character, incapable of resisting the vicissitudes of life outside my own country. To travel in search of success required a mind that was always on the lookout. You can't look back once you've stepped into the wrong river. You need to swim with a strong stroke, and then swim some more to reach the shore.

Leaving means, first of all, being able to fly with your own wings. To know how to land on a branch and continue the flight the next day all the way to the new land, the land that pushed the migrant to leave his footprints far behind in order to encounter a different place, an unknown place . . .

Could I leave? Fly with my own wings? I wasn't certain. I was used to living with my parents. I could count on a roof over my head there and meals. That's how I could nestle in my laziness all day long without having to answer to anyone.

To my mind, France was not a good refuge for a dormouse or snails. I compared it to a world where the clocks were set ahead and where it was necessary to continually catch up with time, without a break, the only way to live. France needed quick, well-informed, resourceful people like Moki. France needed *go-getters*. Quick people, ready to bounce back from inextricable situations as swiftly as a pond mosquito.

I didn't fit that profile . . .

I will remember.

It's here and now that I have to crack open the shell in an effort to remember. Cast aside the night that blurs my vision. Scrape the dirt, find tracks, dust them off, and set them aside so I can put things back where they belong. It might be too late afterwards . . .

In the beginning, there was the name: Moki.

I don't summon the name Préfet, the man that I knew through his go-between, a little later, when I was already on the rue du Moulin-Vert. I won't summon his name. Préfet. I will have time to remember him. He's not getting out of things this way. All I'll need to do is blow on the embers of reminiscence. I will see his face reappear exactly as I saw it that day, in Moki's presence. I will instantly remember that warm handshake, his shifty eyes, and the smell of alcohol . . .

For the moment all I see is Moki.

He is the one at the beginning of the whole thing. I'm sure that our lifelines are crossed. That my own personality was blurred and faded to his advantage. That we have the same breath, the same aspirations, the same fate. The same fate? Yes, so how is it that he doesn't find himself in here with me?

And what if I were only his shadow? If I were only his double? I've asked myself that sometimes. We don't look anything like each other. At least not physically. He is taller than me. Older, too. He's a little heavier than me right now. Me, I stayed puny, despite the dishes made with semolina and potato starch that certain compatriots advised me to eat as soon as I arrived in France, in the hope that this skinny body would gain a few kilos and stop tarnishing the image of our country in the eyes of real Parisians: the men with chubby cheeks and white skin, who cut an elegant figure.

No, Moki and I bear no physical resemblance. I lived like his shadow. I was always behind him.

Especially in the days preceding my journey. I was nothing but a shadow. A shadow is nothing by itself. It needs a presence and a virgin surface on which to print its outline. Sometimes a shadow wants to make a big mistake. It wants to take the initiative. I know that. But a shadow molts at its own risk and peril.

I was Moki's shadow.

He was the one who created me. In his own image. His manner of living bankrolled my dreams. A way of living that I will not forget . . .

—☙—

I remember the many trips he made home while I still hadn't set foot in France. The white man's country had changed his life. Something had shifted; there was an undeniable metamorphosis. He was no longer the frail young man about whom we used to say, if he's as thin as a dry stalk of lantana, it's because he ate standing up and slept on top of an old mat. There was a yawning gap. It wasn't the same Moki.

He was robust, radiant, and in full bloom. I could take note of this, with a tinge of bitterness, because his parents' home was next door to our own. This intimacy compelled me to see his comings and goings over the years. I studied his doings and his gestures with a magnifying glass. France had transformed him. It had chiseled his habits and prescribed another way of life for him. We took note of him with envy.

According to Moki, a Parisian should not live in a hovel like his father's any longer—a shack made from mahogany planks topped by a corrugated sheet metal roof. Their hut was at the edge of a gully, just before the main street. Stunned passersby wondered by what miracle this home had survived the storms during the rainy season. It's not as if Moki's father was indifferent to the dilapidated state of his home. On the contrary, many years before, taking courage in his own two hands, the old man began building another house. This one would be solid, like the one he dreamed of having before retirement. He bought sand, gravel, and a few bags of cement. And that's not all. He had to pay the labor costs and provide for the workers' needs. Back home, skilled workers were fed and paid in *red wine from France,* invited into your home in the evening with their apprentices, for you to serve their every need with your body and soul. It was the owner who had to kowtow, to wait on them hand and foot, and to beg them for months on end. The numbskulls that challenged the way things were done watched their own projects drag on for ages.

Moki's father was one of the latter.

First of all, he could not convince this union of slackers to drastically change their methods of work. The most obvious reason was mainly because of his cash flow. Without financial means, his best intentions were translated into pathetic and laughable creations. He simply piled up rows of bricks and traced the foundation. He quickly ran out of steam. His pockets emptied sooner than expected. He didn't know which moneylender to turn to. They all slammed the door in his face. His hidebound workers would not work for credit. The work came to a halt. The old man threw in the towel. And so he

began to experience the nagging headaches of small propri-
etors who abandon their projects before completion.

Bricks didn't reach their destination. He counted on starting the work again someday, so he outlined his lot by piling
one brick on top of another. He filled his Sundays—the day
for small projects in the courtyard—by counting his bricks.
He gathered and cemented together any bricks that had come
loose. He underestimated the gangs that worked at night: some
youths and other builders or future owners of solid homes
who needed only two or three bricks to finish a facade, a window, a stairway, or water well.

Over time, the old man's enclosure shrank, becoming smaller
and more confined. His goods, if they hadn't been stolen from
him, were found in the street. Drivers of big trucks with bad
brakes used them to brace their vehicles in place. And to top it
off, greenish foam coated the bricks during the rainy season.

One day, he finally flew into a rage and went from house
to house to complain and utter threats about this behavior,
which in his opinion was a deliberate plot to keep him from
finishing the construction of the most beautiful villa in the
neighborhood . . .

We saw that it was Moki, during one of his trips back home,
who decided to resume construction. The Parisian surprised
his father. He surprised us. None of us had ever seen such an
industrious undertaking in the neighborhood before. He hired
a dozen masons who were enticed to work by getting paid in
advance and in amounts that made our mouths water. They
worked under their own boss from morning until very late at
night by the light of lanterns held by apprentices who swayed
with sleepiness. Moki closely supervised the work. He gave
in to the workers' whims. We thought he even spoiled them.
He picked them up at their homes by car in the morning and
drove each of them right to the front of their own homes at
night. He tipped them every day. At the worksite he congratulated them over a small brick set just so, or even for pushing a
wheelbarrow of sand from a little further away. He established
a father and son relationship with the oldest, the lead worker.

This one called him *"my son"* and Moki responded *"my father."* He knew how to find that man's soft spot and stroke his ego.

"My throat is dry, *my son. . . ."*

"My father, I'll bring you some *red wine from France."*

It didn't take long to see the results.

After two and a half months, we woke up in front of an immense white villa. The doors and shutters were painted green. We were all bedazzled. We had no idea that those facades, those columns, the beams and paving stones, would fit together and turn into something so stunning. The whole thing developed the way a puzzle is pieced together. Bricks were lifted and broken in two or three pieces for the foundation; the apprentices rolled barrels of water from the river to the site; bags of cement were torn open with pointed shovels; fine-grained sand and small stones were brought every other day by a dump truck belonging to the Pointe-Noire township; a hammer blow here; the strike of a pick there; the planing of a wood plank; a pinch of pliers on that ironwork; a coat of paint on the doors and windows; sawing rafters from limbs of trees famed for their strength to guarantee a solid roof. These workers were simultaneously carpenters, architects, cabinetmakers, ironworkers, plumbers, and well diggers. They worked on an assembly line.

One thing led to another, and the house was born.

There it was, in front of us. We could study it and get a measure of the toil of those workers who outdid themselves throughout that period of time. An immense villa. There it stood, majestic, on all four sides. Its aluminum tiles glistened in the sun's rays. It stood out from far away and was taller than the nearby shacks that were nothing more than a Capernaum whose disorder was an eyesore, like a favela. There were two worlds. One belonged to the Moki family and the other to the rest of the neighborhood.

This sense of the dichotomy of these two worlds grew sharper when Moki installed electricity and a water pump on their lot. Houses with lighting and access to potable water were rare. Installing this water pump proved useful for the neighborhood. We paid a modest sum of money on days when we filled two or three casks of water. Young people hung out in the evening on the main street in front of the villa to take advantage of the light and talk the night away until Moki's father came out and put an end to that.

—◊—

There were more surprises in store for us . . .

A year after the villa was built, we saw two Toyotas arrive. Moki had chartered and sent them from France so his family could make a profit off them as taxis. That protected the family from utter destitution.

Moki's father was a humble and energetic man. He was short, and that bothered him. We could tell by the jokes he made about tall people, the butt of his jokes, and by the overblown pride he showed when he reminded all those tall forgetful people that he, a tiny little man, barely 160 centimeters, had brought a tall son into the world, a very, very tall son, some 170 centimeters, he insisted, according to Moki. We would fire back that it takes two to make a baby, and the obvious explanation was that his wife was taller than he was.

His modest height was, however, largely offset by a headstrong and stubborn personality and a serious, sepulchral voice. This voice made everyone think he was wise, even apart from his gray beard and bald shiny head, the few strands of hair salvaged from baldness could be counted on the fingers of one hand. He usually dressed in traditional multicolored clothes and rode around on a *pedal* bike. The old man saw his life change in one fell swoop. He was never himself again. It was as if he had followed a calling. His social promotion caught everyone off guard. It was like an unobstructed arrow in flight: he was put on the village council and shortly thereafter unanimously elected its president. His elevation did, of course, cause a bit of grumbling among elders in the neighborhood. But they raised their opposition in the shadows, in the talk shops, not out in the open in the neighborhood where the old man waved his ceremonial cane to demand silence.

We didn't dare confront him. He was blatant in his insistence that it wasn't his gray beard or voice of a baritone gospel singer that got him nominated in such haste to the presidency of the village council. Quite a few old-timers had vied ceaselessly for this honorary position, and their beards were as white, if not whiter, than his. Some of them had stopped shaving the moment their first white hair appeared, and they ostentatiously trailed their beards in the public square like prophets that arrived too late in a world where the gods themselves were reduced to going door-to-door, identity card in hand, instead of their disciples and saints doing it for them. Something else was needed to convince the influential people in the neighborhood. Presidential candidacies are serious business in the village. The way candidates settled accounts had left bad memories in people's minds. According to ancestral beliefs, old people frequently appear at night through the medium of dreams. One elder steps into another's dream by breaking and entering. It's a merciless battle in this netherworld where there are no women or children. The loser's sleep could cost him a one-way ticket to the tomb. So when one could find grounds for agreement, one chose the path of conciliation. The most prudent elders preferred not to take the risk and waited until they were chosen for the throne without any competition. Wasn't this the case with Moki's father?

He wasn't the dean of these Methuselahs. He needed something else to discourage the voracious appetites of those who had waited in line for his post for at least a quarter century. What else? A son who lived in France, for instance, a Parisian. The candidacy of a father of such a son was powerful in itself. Other arguments weighed in his favor: Moki's father was aware of everything going on in France. That was his trump card. Moreover, he had had the chance to attend the colonial school when the teachers—real teachers, he said—were recruited in the middle of the second grade, against their wishes. They tossed you out to go teach in an isolated backwater in the brush. It was a national duty. For Moki's father, to have made it to the second grade in his first year was a point of pride, a

feat that no one of his era had equaled. He wrote and read
French fluently. He could have been a teacher if his parents
had supported him for one more year. In his day there was
only one primary school in the entire south of the country. It
was fifty-two kilometers from Louboulou, the village where he
was born. You went there on foot. You stayed for one week in
a boarding school that accepted only the best students or those
whose parents knew a village leader or a white man. Mothers
and fathers brought food to their children. Alas, after a few
years, squeezed dry by their considerable sacrifices of money
and food, they gave in and asked their children to hightail it
back to the fields to work with them. That's how that type of
education stopped for Moki's father. He picked up a machete
and a hoe and put himself in the service of his parents.

After that, he did what other youth of his generation did
and followed the current of rural exodus. He made his way
to this neighborhood where the closest city, Pointe-Noire,
was fifty kilometers away. He had been living here for some
forty years with his four children and his wife. He worked,
variously, as "boy," then postman and receptionist at Victory
Palace, a French hotel in the city center. His level of education put him above all the other council members who were
for the most part illiterate. During council meetings he spoke
about France—a country he had never visited. He was capable
of reciting to the village council the names of all the kings and
presidents sequentially from the Second Empire of Napoleon
III up to the present, without faltering. He especially liked
General de Gaulle (*Digol* was how he pronounced it) and he
held forth, as if he had been there himself, about how the
General came to Brazzaville in the 1940s and organized a conference in that city with the Algerian Committee. The out-
come of this conference included a plan for a new organization
of the French colonies in black Africa. Moki's father told the
story of this fragment of history at every meeting of the village
council: "General *Digol* was tall. Very tall. A little taller than
Moki," he said. "That's the reason that I gave my son Moki
'Charles' as his first name."

Somebody heckled that the General was quite a bit taller than Moki. He shot back that he knew the General better than anyone, and that people could challenge him on all the French presidents except the General.

"That one, he's mine . . ."

—∿—

Moki's father was aware of his growing influence. The reverence people paid him began to make him lose his head. He wasted no time in adopting the latest fashions. He cast aside all his traditional clothing and preferred to wear clothes *straight from Paris.* From that time on, he wore gray trousers made of virgin wool, well pressed with sharp pleats. No belt, but tricolor suspenders (blue, white, and red), a white dress shirt, a black fedora, and the kind of good black shoes you wear to church. Suddenly he looked like the American blues singer John Lee Hooker. He strolled around the neighborhood, chest out, head held high, both hands in his pockets. Above all, you really needed to see him on his bicycle. He rode slowly, stopping to greet everyone he met at an intersection. Without any prompting, he gave everyone the latest news on Moki. He took out a letter, a postcard. He said that his son had just written him *"a very long letter written in French from France, in the French of Guy de Maupassant himself!"* "What's new?" he'd ask, as if someone had posed the question. "My son is doing fine. The only thing is that it's the middle of winter there right now, you know, winter is the season when the trees are in mourning, the birds are few and far between, the streets trail sadness, and even the white people stuff themselves into warm, heavy clothing. Ah, the snow is . . . how I can explain it to you? It's like the foam on top of a beer, but a little firmer than that. When it snows, the roads over there are useless. It's not easy to stop a car. The cold can kill you. You have to consume a lot of hot drinks and not stick your nose outside . . ."

He recited these words like a child who had really memorized his lesson. He knew how to keep the crowd that was listening to him from leaving. Most importantly, he did not

forget to tell everyone the exact date his son would return
home . . .

—ᴍ—

We knew it. Moki wouldn't be coming home except during
the vacations in the dry season, between July and September.
That was party time. The liveliest time in the country.
Everything suddenly happened so fast. The days, the weeks,
the months ran by at a dizzying pace. The tree of time doesn't
let us have our fill savoring its fruits. Was it because this was
the time of year we looked forward to the most? Of course.
In the neighborhood, the smallest brouhaha turned into a
mob scene. A brawl was the best excuse for everyone to come
together in the street. We went out, not to put an end to the
scuffle but in hopes that the show would last longer.

When I think back on it now with a little distance, this
unquenchable thirst for relaxation sprang from unimaginable
situations. Funerals were no longer the lugubrious scenes they
were known to be. We laughed and we burst into giggles more
than we cried. We played chess and checkers and cards. We
drank beer, palm wine, and maize alcohol all night long. We
arranged to meet each other there, just a few meters from the
corpse, behind the palm leaf hut where the distressed and suffering family cried and couldn't do anything about it. The loss
was nothing but a pretext. It was completely justified that we
almost begged heaven to take the soul of an old person every
week so that we could count on a moment to get together
and collectively blow off some steam. The population in the
neighborhood grew tenfold. And on top of that there were
vacationers from the city and nearby villages.

We all knew the latest. Moki was going to come back from
Paris. His father didn't keep the secret from anyone. People in
the neighborhood had nothing but his son's return on their
lips. We were definitely waiting for the Parisian. That day was a
blessed day. An event. The sudden hustle and bustle of Moki's
parents and brothers proved it. The Parisian's family did not
skimp on anything in preparation. It was time for a lot of work

to be done. Everyone rolled up their sleeves. The courtyard
was swept meticulously. Part of the street in front of the home
was sprayed with water three times a day. Not a single leaf
from the mango trees was left on the ground. The Parisian's
room, which looked out on the main street, was fixed up. The
trunks of trees around the property were repainted. The two
taxis were washed every night. A small table wrought of tropical vines was placed under the mango tree in the center of the
courtyard. That's where the Parisian would eat his meals. He
would eat *outdoors*. The real reason was so that he ate in full
view and knowledge of everyone. These little details were of
great importance to Moki's father. He said that his son would
not eat like the lowliest village peasant. According to him,
peasants swallowed big pieces of manioc with a little bit of
salted fish, really just a very little bit, the size of a child's finger.
Then they drank two liters of water. What mattered was that
their stomachs were full. Moki's father laid out in detail the
meals fit for his son to eat: he'd have an aperitif, an appetizer,
a main dish, *red wine from France*, cheese, a dessert, and coffee.
Just like in France, *chez Digol* . . .

The old man swung into action and stayed up all night to
get ready for Moki's arrival. He didn't use his bicycle anymore. To save time he got around in one of the two taxis. For
these circumstances he got a chauffeur. He wore his nicest
clothes, which had come *straight from Paris*. He was involved
and took personal responsibility for the shopping that needed
to be done. We knew him as an affable, smiling man, eager to
please his neighbors. He hung all these qualities in his closet
and displayed a remorseless severity.

His chauffeur was no more than a whipping boy. The poor
man endured his every fit of anger. The old man barked con-
tradictory orders. He ordered him to park the car here, then
there, then a little further away, before finally deciding to park
it in the first spot. He ordered him to stay in the car with the
motor running. As soon as the car was moving, Moki's father
dictated to the chauffeur how fast he should drive. He repeat-
edly told him to first shift into gear and then to carefully put

on the brakes. The two men appeared to be driving together. "Turn left! Signal! Beep the horn! Don't give him the right of way. Can't you see that his car is older than ours? Pass that imbecile who's blowing smoke right in my face! Who is that crackpot trying to pass us? Step on it. Don't let him pass you! Come on, I said, go, go, go . . ."

Under the stress of it all, the father of the Parisian aged ten years. Deep wrinkles streaked his face. A big vein that started on his forehead split his head in two. His eyes were red, his eyelids made heavier with black circles and lifeless pockets of skin. He wiped the sweat off his body with his fedora. He shouted himself hoarse, becoming irascible and more bilious as the big day appeared closer on the horizon. He took a calendar, crossed out the days gone by, counted how many were yet to come, underlined *the big day* in red, and scrawled something. He was not the least bit satisfied. Some small detail was missing. He complained. The courtyard wasn't properly swept? He'd have none of it, and after scolding his wife and sons, he grabbed a long-handled broom himself. He stood, straight as an "I," facing his property, his eyes riveted on the mango trees. He kept track of the leaves that fell. He lambasted the trees, promising to cut them down if they persisted in dropping their dead leaves with each ill-tempered gust of wind. That's how his long monologues began. Words had no beginning and no end. A laugh that resonated and made us think he was no longer from this world. At meetings of the village council, the poor dignitaries were at a loss with his recitations about Paris, France, and the bravery of the man of June 18th: "*Digol*, a great man such as him doesn't exist anymore. Men like him, they only come once a century. Indeed, there are even centuries when fate holds back and stockpiles its reserves of great men."

The tenor of the old man's voice conveyed his emotional sincerity. Loyalty sparkled in his eyes, a blind loyalty deeply rooted in the depth of his soul.

"Remember, my friends, *Digol* outright refused the 1940 armistice and the Vichy government. He sent an unforgettable appeal to London to drive forward without reprieve to combat

the Nazis. How can you talk about the Resistance without realizing the stature of this mighty beefwood tree whose head is
crowned with laurels of all the victories he won for the grandeur of France? After that, some youthful ingrates wanted to
stir up trouble for him, to make mountains out of molehills,
in May 1968. They were minuscule groups of students and
union members. There, too, *Digol* showed he was a giant by
leaving the seat of power one year later because those forgetful French people dared to challenge him in a test of strength,
when they rejected a new course he proposed to them with a
referendum . . ."

—⁓—

In the evening, a wreck, his voice gone, the old man ran
a trembling hand over his head, pulled out an armchair covered in leopard skin, and sank into it. He crossed his frail legs,
adjusted his suspenders, filled his pipe, and drew long puffs.

He was already snoring.

His wife, an almost imperceptible silhouette compared with
the old man's strong personality, timidly shook him. The moon
was just above them, round and grand: the dry season had
come.

The son was coming . . .

MOKI HAD ARRIVED.

Disorder in front of their villa. Crowds. The street was swarming with people. The light blazed bright all night long on their lot.

The Parisian's first day back was the day for family members. Even the most distant relative quickly climbed down the branches of the genealogical tree and announced their presence that day. They feared they would miss out on the hypothetical manna Moki brought back if they weren't there. The cautious ones who could not turn up because of illness had their sons represent them. Maternal and paternal uncles, aunts, grandfathers, grandmothers, i.e., everyone belonging to the same villages as Moki's father and mother turned up. Some—very few—brought presents: a chicken, a pig, or a sack of peanuts. The animals all capered about here and there in a concert of piercing cackles and grunts.

Other family members, the majority, came with their arms dangling at their sides, counting on the right of primogeniture, or how closely they were related, which they externalized with familiarities that, in the end, never failed to irritate those in attendance. The family members sat in a small congregation in the courtyard, one after another, beggars for the Parisian's favors.

He listened to each and every one's complaints, agreeing with this one, reprimanding that one, offering further consolation. At a certain point he got bored. He watched the birds perched on the mango tree. He squashed flies on the table. He was somewhere else. But he couldn't leave this gathering without running the risk of offending the family.

And so it was that a paternal uncle, jumping from one subject to another, complained about the past year's bad harvest to explain why he had arrived empty-handed, while a misty-eyed grandfather took his turn to explain that he had been in Adolphe-Cissé Hospital for a month without a single visit from the family members gathered together today. Scolding sounds grew louder. He was made to understand that this was not the time for an outpouring of bilious arguments. They would settle all of that amongst themselves. An aunt wanted to speak privately with Moki, it seemed, to share a dream about him that came back to her again and again each time the Parisian left for France . . .

Moki's father managed this whole group with his watchful eyes. He couldn't throw them out, even if he thought they were a nuisance. To chase them like flies would jinx his son. Among our people, one family member's success was not the business of one or two people. It had to benefit the entire clan in the broadest way possible. The old man required no reminder of the innumerable examples of egotistical parents who brought the curse upon themselves: the death of their sons and the funerals that not a single person attended. Everyone knows the popular saying about this. *"Money has never mourned the dead."* Moki's father was mindful of traditions. He respected them scrupulously. For him, hospitality was the highest principle. Leave the door open all day long. Prepare to feed more mouths than live in your house. Expect visitors at any moment. Don't ask them foolish questions like: "Have you already eaten?" Instead, tell them: "Have a seat. We will bring you food and fresh water. . . ."

To the question, *"Have you already eaten?"* the majority of visitors would reply *"yes"* with a sallow smile, mumbled under a mustache. They would stifle themselves, despite the hunger that knotted their stomachs. This torture spoke to their desire not to debase themselves by responding in the negative to that question. Don't be mistaken by *"I've already eaten"*—you have to hear the resentment of the person with the lump in their throat. Better to die of hunger than to give a humiliating response, even if no food had passed their lips the night before. They leave, red-eyed with upset, their stomachs burbling with uninterrupted sounds. They consider themselves defeated, ridiculed, diminished like vulgar dogs that come home with their tails between their legs. They would immediately go out and say that they were offered nothing to eat, not even a glass of fresh water, and thus a family conflict would be born that could last several generations . . .

The old man also did not forget that according to popular belief in the country, luck and success were just the achievement of blessings upon all family members, even the most distant. It was an obligation to support these parasites sometimes. They would eventually leave. And don't ask them when they would be coming back. Such a question would infuriate them forever. They would immediately grab their bags and shake the dust off their shoes in front of the home as a curse. So Moki's father put up with it. He opened his door, took out old straw mattresses, and laid them on the ground himself. Meals were prepared in big aluminum pots. But a slight tension was visible in the old man's face. He camouflaged it. He'd pass by and get involved in a vehement argument, turn away from it, go back to his leopard skin chair, cross his legs, and fill his pipe.

He smoked with his eyes closed. Yet for all that, he didn't sleep. He returned to serve his guests beer and *red wine from France*. They drank, shouted themselves hoarse, told tales of the Parisian's childhood. An aunt, tipsy from palm wine, recalled that her nephew defecated on her when he was four months old. An uncle boasted that he had seen Moki's first tooth. A distant cousin insisted that they had played marbles and soccer with a ball made of rags that Moki had known how to make back then.

In the evening, people nestled together in the salon to sleep. Indeed, half the family spent the night there. Especially those

who had come from very far away. The others went back to
their homes and returned very early the next morning . . .

On the second day, conversations were exhausted. They
touched on the weather, on how to shell peanuts quickly, to
let the cattle graze during the dry season, about the morals of
these young girls who came back from the big cities with skirts
that left their whole derrières hanging out. These conversations continued in absolute unanimity. They got bogged down.
Jokes and pleasantries no longer captured anyone's imagination. Instead, those assembled watched the Parisian's every
gesture. They witnessed in silence. This weighty silence meant
that one expected things would finally turn to serious matters.

Who didn't think so?

Then Moki began handing out little gifts. The family was
attentive to the distribution. Everyone looked out of the corner of their eye at what the other had received to compare
it with their own present. The fake coughing of an impotent
patriarch meant that he felt he had not done as well as he
should have and the distribution should be reconsidered. The
Parisian reviewed his prize and added two or three trinkets.
The old man exhaled joyfully. For Moki, the distribution was
a complicated and dangerous exercise. His father intervened
in advance, with complete discretion. He alerted Moki, armed
with his experience:

"Pay attention to what you give the old people. Those
people are waiting for just one false move to stir up the ashes.
Do you remember the story of Kombo's son, who died because
he didn't offer a torch to his old uncle? Of course, some people
would think that's a ridiculous gift, but he would have used
that torch for hunting and to keep away evil spirits when the
shadows of the night send us the devils from neighboring
villages . . ."

In the end, everyone left with *a little something from France*
and gave thanks, in the first instance to the Parisian's father,
and then to him, while wishing him good luck. The same
phrase was oft repeated:

"Thanks a lot, Moki. Until next year . . ."

The Parisian's father could finally breathe; the nuisances had scampered off.

He blessed his son, hugged him with his legs, touched his head, and asked him to hug the ground. This did not surprise the Parisian. Every year, every dry season, the same ritual was repeated. The ritual of luck and success.

—〰—

Moki had arrived.

The first thing we noticed was the color of his skin. Nothing at all like ours, poorly cared for, devoured by the scorching sun, oily and as black as manganese. His was extraordinarily white. He argued that they didn't have winter over there for nothing. Later, in France, I learned that he applied hydroquinone products to his entire body. The young people of the country who knocked themselves out in their irreversible blindness to ape Parisians made do with cheap products made in Africa like Ambi Red and Ambi Green. The results were not the same. They didn't come close to the brilliant skin of a Parisian. The suffocating heat of the country accelerated side effects. The imitators got slapped with allergies, red spots, and blood clots on their faces.

Moki's pace was nimble, light-footed. One would have said it was the sound of a cotton ball falling on the floor. He must have walked in slow motion, suspended. Every one of his movements was detailed elegance. No gesture, no movement, was excessive. Everything was planned down to the nearest millimeter. This elegance disconcerted the young girls in the neighborhood. They spoke of nothing but the Parisian. They flocked together on the main street to watch him go by, offering him a timid and reverent hello. They spied on him, followed his comings and goings, guessing what he did with his time . . .

During the first week, Moki passed his time sitting under the mango tree in the courtyard, there where his father had set up a dining table. The father and son talked, looked around together at what the house needed. The old man wore an expression of infinite happiness. He wore new clothes, tried using a television outside—one of the gifts his son had given him. He never left the Parisian. These conversations spread out over at least a week.

Afterwards, Moki's time was spent very simply. Sit under the Mango tree. Go out when he was invited by the neighborhood girls.

In the morning, he read newspapers from Paris that he had brought back with him from the North: *Ici Paris, Paris Match, Le Parisien* . . . He stayed in his silk robe with taffeta motifs. Young men from the neighborhood, his childhood friends, came by to cut his hair. He paid for these services with things from Paris. And not just any odd thing! Moki thanked them with little Paris Métro maps. They were jubilant. Of course, they didn't understand these tangled itineraries, these numbered lines that were so intertwined that one would have said it was a hydrographic map of China. They surprised the Parisian himself. In fact, certain natives described the Métro lines with unequaled talent, station by station, to the point that you would have thought they had stayed in Paris. Others took pseudonyms after the names of the stations. One dubbed himself Saint-Placide. Another, Strasbourg-Saint-Denis. Yet another, Colonel Fabien and Maubert-Mutalité. They added the word "Monsieur" to these pseudonyms. *Monsieur Saint-Placide, Monsieur Strasbourg-Saint-Denis, Monsieur Colonel Fabien, Monsieur Maubert-Mutalité.*

Moki also supplied them with unused Métro passes. They glued their photographs on them and wowed the more naïve girls.

The local heat bothered the Parisian now. Even this moderate dry season sun. He didn't eat manioc or foufou anymore, the basic foodstuffs of the country that he grew up on. He preferred bread. Manioc and foufou had no dietary virtue, he said. He looked anxiously at everything he put in his mouth.

We admired his speaking style. He spoke *French French.* The famous French of Guy de Maupassant, whom his father alluded to. He pretended that our tongues were predestined to mispronounce the words. Thus we didn't speak real French. What we considered to be French, with our rustic accent, a dry, coarse, and jerky accent, was not in fact French. It was an unintelligible string of *firofonfon naspa*, the French of a former little black soldier and pretentious collector of medals. We listened to him with pleasure, dumbfounded and won over. Just to hear him speak was an intense moment. It was he who taught us that even those imbeciles who presented the television and radio news in our country didn't speak the real French of France. He, Moki, didn't grasp what they were telling us.

"There's a big difference between speaking *in* French and speaking *French*," he claimed, without developing his point.

We acquiesced. Amongst ourselves, the game was who could imitate him the best. We tried. Nobody succeeded, not even his three brothers, the oldest of whom was a civil servant in the Post and Telecommunications office in the center of Pointe-Noire. And then there were the word choices. The Parisian used *big words*. You had to listen to all those words that pleasantly caress the ear and that were likely to amaze the listener. And between a simple, more precise word and a grandiose word, he opted for the latter, no matter what it meant . . .

Moki didn't move around on foot.

He would not debase himself by getting caught in the sand and the muddy streets like a vulgar native. No, that was out of the question. He would not lower himself down to that level, especially because he owned two taxis. He commandeered one. The chauffeur, the same one used by his father, puffed out his chest and swaggered. He proclaimed from every rooftop that he had been chosen to be the Parisian's driver. The king was no longer his cousin. We saw the car scour the neighborhood all day long. The chauffeur did not allow Moki to open or shut the door. He took a devilish pleasure in performing his duties. His zeal impelled him to turn on the trouble lights to announce the presence of the Parisian in the car. He played music in the background, lowered the windows, and made the vehicle dance by hitting the brakes heavily and regularly. For no reason at all, he honked the horn and yelled insults at those in his way. He thought he came first, no matter what. He didn't slow down when approaching intersections. When Moki got out of the car to go into a West African's boutique around the corner, the zealous chauffeur took that time to use a cloth and cleaning product. He nervously set himself upon the car windows until he achieved a brilliance he deemed impeccable. He dashed away from the car to contemplate it from a distance. He returned at the same speed, his eyes fixed on a spot he detected on the windshield. He vigorously sprayed a hefty dose of product and polished the glass while uttering swear words against himself. Everything was just right if he didn't bang the glass with his fist.

Moki returned.

In an outpouring of obsequiousness, the chauffeur fell back two steps, then four, so as to not walk in front of the Parisian. He scrambled for the door, opened it, grinning ear to ear. He took off at top speed, not without having accomplished one of his specialties: a big figure eight in the sand amid a salvo of applause from groupies idling nearby . . .

Moki received visitors. In actual fact, he issued strict instructions to his younger brothers to make sure they selected visitors well. Young girls were spared this unpleasantness. The villa's doors were open to them at all times. They took advantage. They came running. Since they needed a motive to justify their untimely visits, they all said they came to *ask about the latest fashion trends in Paris.* They arrived early in the morning, stayed half the day, going so far as to help Moki's mother do the shopping and cooking, watering and sweeping the courtyard.

It was no longer rare to hear that in a certain street in the neighborhood at a certain hour, young girls fiercely confronted each other, with their claws out, because of the Parisian.

And then there were all those less enterprising ladies, held back by pathological shyness. They were the most fragile. Their feelings languished in the shadows. They didn't dare approach the Parisian. They waited patiently, counting that he would personally take the initiative himself. They could wait forever.

Many girls had photographs of Moki in Paris. They bought these pictures for the price of gold, and sometimes *payment in kind*, according to our hallowed expression.

Who was behind this traffic in photos of the Parisian? His two younger brothers, of course. These two proclaimed themselves their elder brother's spokesmen. They swore by nothing except his name. Only Moki knew the truth about Paris. Other Parisians who were less famous in the country were nothing but vile liars. Moki's brothers were servile. True automatons. They never spoke for themselves anymore. They went ahead and spoke to us about France, to preach to us just like their brother would have done. This devotion on their part was compensated. The Parisian *dressed them*. He offered them clothing he had already worn. The brothers handed them down to each other, one after the next. These outfits were coveted by the neighborhood *show-offs*. They suggested to the Parisian's brothers that they *mine* them. Throughout the country, *mines* consisted of clothes borrowed for a sum of money for a rendezvous or a night out. You'd have to get up early to *mine* these outfits. Demand exceeded supply. The best was to be among the first *miners*, thereby avoiding having to wear this clothing after one of the young neighborhood *show-offs* put them on. Those really in the know reserved a year in advance. The price was high. That was the cost of exclusivity. It wasn't given to just anyone . . .

Moki's brothers took advantage of their brother's reign to impose their own. Every young person that wanted to speak with the Parisian had to go through them. Two inseparable brothers. So inseparable that we dubbed them (secretly, of course) Dupond and Dupont, just like the characters in *The Adventures of Tintin*. Those who took the risk of calling them that aloud definitely compromised their chances of meeting the Parisian someday. The brothers' demands intersected the rhythm of requests. They became unbearable, vain, more royalist than the king, two caliphs in place of one. They scorned

you for saying whatever. They attained the heights of pre-
sumptuousness. They protected their restricted domain, their
private preserve. They strolled near the mango tree in the
courtyard. Or they kept Praetorian Guard outside the door to
their brother's room while he rested. As soon as they heard
him, or thought they heard his cough, both of them went running to investigate the situation. They took turns to make sure
the villa was permanently guarded. Every undesirable male
visitor was forcibly evicted.

The two fierce guardians were overwhelmed. Or rather, they
gave the impression of being so. They were here. They were
there. We didn't see anyone but them anymore. Sometimes
in a taxi with their father, the conductor who lifted his baton
higher and higher to show that he had the situation under
control and to count on him.

Dupond and Dupont each owned a Vélosolex moped. They
rode around, dressed to the nines. They made no secret of
their satisfaction. The false image they projected decrypted
for us the real image they had of themselves. To their eyes,
the neighborhood youth were nothing but poor wretches,
cockroaches who should grovel before their commands. Their
power? They were the blood brothers of the Parisian and
therefore, by ricochet effect, potential Parisians themselves.
The girls understood this. It was better to bury the hatchet
with those two. Otherwise, the brothers would exact conse-
quences when the time came . . .

The girls were ready to drop everything to nail a rendezvous ahead of their competition. In the interest of getting the
best place in the race and not getting sent back to the end of
the line, they bribed Dupond and Dupont. Those two pleaded
the girl's case with the Parisian. They requested a rendezvous
at a *buvette,* one of those public eateries and watering holes
that were found all over the country. In those places, people
drink, eat, talk, and listen to music outside, seated on stools
around tables. It goes without saying that the girls would get
their money's worth, once Moki agreed to meet them. They
presumed that the fallout would not be negligible. Otherwise,

they contented themselves with a visit to the Parisian's home, where they were welcomed whenever they wanted. But who could see them talking in a house? It was the spectacle that got them to enlist in this way. The *buvette* was the dream location because everyone would see them eating grilled fish and having a drink in the company of the Parisian. These rendezvous were also a godsend for Moki, whose influence rose a notch, speaking of him, of Paris, and of his exploits as a dandy at Aristocrats—a club for young elegant people in the neighborhood, where he had once been president.

Did he tell stories about events that really happened, or was he leading his listener down the garden path? Nobody could answer that question.

—⁓—

The meetings with girls at a *buvette* took place toward late afternoon. The young ladies waited for him for hours. They worried themselves sick with the thought that the Parisian had changed his mind at the last minute and would turn up at a more enticing rendezvous with one of their competitors. Moki arrived without so much as a word of explanation for being late. The girls thanked him profusely. They devoured the Parisian with their eyes and assessed the value of his clothes under their breath. He had a weakness for linen, a fabric about which one said, *"It wears sublimely and crumples divinely."*

During the course of one of these encounters—how could I ever forget it—I was there, at the back of the crowd. The Parisian filled us with wonder. For me, it wasn't the first time. I couldn't help myself and rushed over when I learned that he had been invited to a *buvette* by the girls.

On the day that I'm thinking of, he was dressed in a tailor-made suit by Francesco Smalto. A very see-through shirt allowed you to make out his white skin as soon as he took off his jacket in public. His silk tie was covered in a pattern of miniscule Eiffel Towers. He wore only Weston shoes, and he was the only one in the country to have a pair made of crocodile; one pair cost the equivalent of a minister's salary in our country. His brothers, who accompanied him, swam in roomy outfits like the *Zouaves* wore, those soldiers in the French infantry formed in Algeria in 1831, who wore big puffy breeches in resplendent colors.

To wear their big brother's pants, Dupond and Dupont used shrewd tricks. First they put on several pairs of breeches and then wore the pants on top of them. Is this pair longer than the other? If it wasn't right, they fashioned their own makeshift hems with paperclips.

Dupond and Dupont played a leading role in pulling off these rendezvous successfully. Each one had a specific task. One of them opened the car door. The other held an umbrella over the Parisian's head. Not a ray of sun on his fragile skin. As soon as he was out of the car and aware that all eyes were upon him, he put on what could have been a walk down a fashion runway, to the great delight of the fanatics sitting in the *buvette*. He unbuttoned his jacket, handed it to one of his brothers behind him. Under the see-through shirt, his skin looked brighter, almost pale, without any irritation or the other severe allergies borne by local imitators. This metamorphosis stupefied the crowd. The Parisian hitched his pants up all the way to his belly button. The gesture was stiff, contrived, and rehearsed, in order to show off his socks, which matched his tie. One of his brothers handed him Emmanuelle Khanh sunglasses, not to wear them but to pose them lightly on his forehead. A hail of bravos ensued. The girls forgot their long hours of waiting patiently and gushed frenetically.

Meanwhile, Moki's car was parked in front of the *buvette* with the zealous driver inside. He pretended to kill time flipping through a *Tex Willer* comic book, which he kept hidden in the glove compartment. From time to time he would get out of the car and lean back on the automobile, fancying himself the star of the day, too. He waited. He waited. He was happy, in his way. He didn't ask himself a lot of questions, confining himself to gathering the crumbs thrown on the floor for him. His motto was simple, sharp, and clear: *"The king's dog is the king of dogs."*

His boss didn't push him into the limelight. All you had to do
was look at him closely to realize that. The tie he wore didn't
come from Paris. He must have bought it from a Senegalese
street peddler in the marketplace. It hung in a coil like a small
intestine cut to pieces with a table knife. It was buckled as if he
had washed it in soap and cold water and ironed it before it had
dried. As for the knot, it was as big as a fist and gave sufficient
information about the fight he had had in front of his mirror to
put it on. And the rest of his outfit? The chauffeur was stuffed
into a jacket whose sleeves barely encompassed his hairy fore-
arms. Yellow stains from ironing marked the underside of the
garment. He must have only ironed it in those spots. He wore
a short-sleeved shirt, so it didn't extend beyond the sleeves of
his jacket. It was white in name only. His right shoe was more
worn than his left. It was easy to see that this was the foot that
titillated his favorite object every day: that little button, the
car's accelerator. This was also the foot he used to keep the beat
when he listened to music outside in front of the taxi, while
waiting for a client to request his service.

He was there. He waited. He would wait. A brother of the
Parisian thought of him from time to time and brought him a
bottle of Primus beer. The chauffeur quenched his thirst. But
under no circumstances was he to move away from the automobile . . .

A conversation started up between Moki and the girls
around one of the tables in the *buvette*. Paris was the subject
of the meeting. After nonsensical explanations about the division of arrondissements in Paris, Moki faced perplexed looks.
Nobody understood what he had said. He summoned one of
his brothers. The latter bent down, agreed with every word
his boss, the Parisian, said, and then went toward the taxi.
He came back with a stack of photo albums in his arms and
placed the heavy pile in front of his elder brother. He resumed
his place, two tables away, where, with his other brother, he
followed the events unfolding step by step. The photographs
of Moki in Paris were passed from hand to hand while he
continued to tell tales rendered less dubious by these images.

He went on to explain that you could eat dinner on the Eiffel Tower, that he himself went there on weekends with friends, that he used to have a big apartment with a view of this monument built by Gustave Eiffel, that every morning, while brushing his teeth, he had to put up with that view, that he became sick of it, that he moved to a new apartment and since then lived in the fourteenth arrondissement, near the Tour Montparnasse. He revealed that there were several unoccupied rooms in his apartment and he had gone to look for compatriots at the Gare du Nord railway station to offer them housing, homeless compatriots who hadn't had a permanent address in years, but they bitterly deceived him. They urinated in his sink and hid food in his closet . . .

The captivated audience laughed heartily. Moki was encouraged by heads nodding approval. He didn't pause again. The throngs in front of the *buvette* confirmed the relevance of his words. Curious passersby stopped, listened for a few minutes, and took seats without being invited. Dupond and Dupont pushed them toward the back of the *buvette*. Questions flew from all sides, like at a press conference. One question that had become a classic was asked: "Have you already slept with a *real* white woman?"

"What's a *real* white woman?" Of course, the imperturbable Parisian bounced back into action. "Moreover, I'll tell you that it's nothing like women here; over there, they're ready to wash your feet, to run your bath, and to feed you like a baby. At first, I only went out with white women to snub our colored sisters who, from the moment they arrive in Paris, act as if they were god knows who. With a white person, whether it's yes or no . . ."

This words instigated muttering. The Parisian polished his sunglasses before responding to the next question:

"So, you know everything about Paris?"

The question came from the back of the *buvette*. The person who posed the question was tucked in a dark corner. He was pinpointed immediately, thanks to someone at a neighboring table batting her eyes and nodding insistently in the direction

of Dupond and Dupont. Moki made a forced laugh. His sincerity and trust had just been questioned. At least that's how
he understood the question. He made light of the impudent
effrontery. The audience concurred that it was an idiotic question. Only an imbecile could have asked that.

Reaction wasn't long in coming. Moki's brothers split the
crowd in two, stepping on a few fingers and toes, hoisting
themselves on the shoulders and legs of others, and flung
themselves on the imposter, knocking over several tables in
the process. They ignored the bottles and glasses that crashed
to the floor, having only one objective: to throw out the
troublemaker.

That's when Moki intervened. "Leave it be," he said, in a
falsely pacified voice. "I'm going to answer him to shut his
trap for good. I have nothing to hide from you. All of you
here know, I suppose, what a village is, right? Well, that's it!
Everyone in Paris knows me, and everyone calls me by my
name when I pass by in the street: Charles Moki. Himself. I
was one of the best *sapeurs*[1] in the capital, the city of elegance. I
made my mark at the Rex Club in Paris. I silenced all my competitors. So ask me real questions. Moreover, I defy any one
of you here: if God gives you the chance to see Paris someday,
that magnificent city, I'm warning you that you will not get
anywhere without my help, I guarantee you that. Paris is in
my pocket. I know that city, and nobody knows it better than
me. The little fool who was moaning in the back over there
has no chance of seeing Paris, I'll tell you that!" . . .

Derisive laughter.

Evidently, the imbecile had split the scene by himself, on
tiptoes, seeing that Moki had raised his voice. What followed
were questions the Parisian deemed interesting. He whole-
heartedly congratulated those who posed the questions.
Someone had asked him, "How do you become *Parisian?*"

"Good question! What's your name?"

---

1. SAPE: Society for Ambiancers and Persons of Elegance.

The young man stammered his first name. Moki took his time before satisfying his sycophants. "I'm going to give you an honest answer. People have a tendency to get everything mixed up. You don't become a Parisian overnight or because you live in Paris. Don't hold your breath. It requires patience, time, but also talent. First, you have to win over people back home and then take on the City of Light, Paris. Me, that's how I started. I grew up with my group of friends, Benos, Préfet, and Boulou, who are still in Paris with me, real fighters. Back then, we formed a club that was headquartered here in the neighborhood, just behind the meeting hall of the village council headed by my father. Our club was called the Aristocrats, and back then I was the president . . .

Moki interrupted himself to assess the effect of his story. He allowed the murmuring to go on so that he could catch his breath and swallow a few mouthfuls of beer. He shot a glance in the direction of his car. The chauffeur was smiling. A sign that his patience had no limits. He was surrounded by bottles of beer. He was bug-eyed drunk. He belched loudly.

Moki recovered his strength and chased the cats purring in his throat.

In a didactic tone, he continued: "Our club, the Aristocrats, was the most prestigious club in this country. Do the math—that's where the real Parisians came from. We knew how to organize. We knew everything about Paris, fashion, the attitudes, everyday life. I was the one who spoke about French culture. I'm not boasting, I had no credentials because, don't forget, I went as far as high school in my studies, even though I failed my baccalaureate in literature twice. I read a lot of French authors that you don't know: Guy de Maupassant and his tales that evoke the life of peasants in Normandy, love stories and adventure tales; André Gide and his *Travels in the Congo;* Albert Camus and *The Plague;* Victor Hugo's *Les Misérables.* I amazed the girls by reciting verses of Lamartine's *Poetic Meditations* and Alfred de Vigny's *Death of a Wolf,* which is, in my opinion, one of the most beautiful poems in French literature. My father worked in a hotel run by French people and visited by conscripts and aid workers, the Victory Palace. He brought books, newspapers, and magazines back to the house that the French had thrown in the garbage after reading them. Me, thanks to that, I taught myself. I paid attention to everything having to do with the City of Light. We learned to speak slang through the *San Antonio* detective stories. My father was opposed to me reading them, he who would have liked to have been a teacher. We passed them around secretly. That language elevated us above other youth who were in fact nothing but old-young.

"What we were most preoccupied with was how people dressed, la *sape,* and to leave for Paris one day. School became a handicap. It turned us away from our goal. We had a box, and each one of us would deposit a fixed amount we agreed upon each month. With that money, we would go to the big market at Pointe-Noire to buy flea market clothes that came from Paris. Don't get me wrong, even in the country market, you had to have an eye and especially taste. We didn't buy just any clothing. There was linen, alpaca, crepe. Jeans were prohibited. An Aristocrat did not wear jeans. Those things were made for mechanics and plumbers, not for people like us with a fashion aesthetic. We also bought suits made of leather and buckskin. These threads, acquired with the help of our dues, were the property of the club, of all the Aristocrats. We wore them on the weekend according to a collectively discussed distribution plan. Young people from nearby neighborhoods came to *mine* them. Money from this *mine* enabled us to buy other clothes. We owned mopeds, like my younger brothers today. A moped is associated with the image of a dandy. You radiate an allure when you ride the bike. The discrete allure and marvelous contours are made for everyone who loves elegance. A little push of the pedal and the motor hummed: Titit . . . Titit . . . Titit . . .

"There were a lot of us walking Indian file with our Solex mopeds along Independence Avenue at Pointe-Noire. We weren't called *sapeurs* yet, but *fighters.* This latter term unfortunately had a pejorative side. It inspired brutality, combat, while all we demanded of ourselves was refinement, elegance, and beauty. From *fighters* we went to being called *playboys*. But that all sounded too English or American. Today we are *sapeurs*, and so much the better. Far from putting out fires, we love ambiance, the beautiful lifestyle, and we admire beautiful creatures such as those surrounding me here. Is it because the word *sapeurs* is going out of style little by little that we are now called *Parisians?* Clothing is our passport. Our religion. France is the country of fashion because it is the only place in the world where you can judge a book by its cover. That's the truth, believe you me."

Some pushing and shoving at the entrance to the buvette.

Other passersby joined the girls and the curious crammed inside. People argued over places in the back, each one claiming that they had that stool first. An impatient sort demanded silence. Moki took another long sip of beer. His lost look projected him far back in time. Regret furrowed his brow.

He went on, in a sad voice: "Back when we were called *fighters* with our Solex, we challenged other clubs in the neighborhood. These challenges were high points for our club. To succeed, the members discussed among themselves the best tactics to use and how to dress for the day of battle. No dissenting voice should make itself known. All the Aristocrats dressed impeccably. For my part, as president, I had a pipe with a gold ring. We learned together how to put on a tie, place a handkerchief in a jacket pocket, walk like a show-off, hold a cigarette, serve and drink from a glass. In short, we learned everything that made us what we are today and all that, I would think, all of you wish to become tomorrow. The club challenges allowed us to test our supremacy.

"We challenged our adversaries on their own turf. To encourage them to answer us, we upset them a bit with our insolence. We treated them as if they were poorly dressed; we told them that they were incapable of dressing Parisian style, incapable of speaking of that city, of expressing themselves in French, of citing from memory the most famous passages from the great French authors. In this regard, if I say to you, *'The earth teaches*

us more about ourselves than do all the books. Because it resists us.
Man discovers himself against the obstacle. But to do so, he needs a
tool . . .' Whose thoughts are these? Saint-Exupéry! *Wind, Sand*
and Stars. Or this verse, too:

> *Folly and error, stinginess and sin*
> *Possess our spirits and fatigue our flesh.*
> *And like a pet we feed our tame remorse*
> *As beggars take to nourishing their lice.*

"It's the famous preface at the beginning of Charles
Baudelaire's *The Flowers of Evil.* We borrowed these books from
the French cultural center to arm ourselves. The challenge
had to be included in an advertisement. We pasted posters
about the challenge on the facades of primary and secondary
schools, putting our posters over the posters of our adversaries. In the end they took the bait and answered us. They stood
up to the challenge. There was no other solution. Ridicule was
no small thing. So they furiously tore down our posters and
replaced them with their own. They considered us poor sports,
dirty, and bugs they would squash as soon as possible. Tension
mounted on both sides. The ingredients for a good challenge
were assembled. The dish was going to be spicy. Very spicy.
Nothing remained but to carry out the act itself.

"Our tactic? First of all, to sound out our adversary's forces.
And so we sent our scouts into the other club's territory.
We had to be *au courant* of what they were going to wear in
order to counter them. From their side, too, there's no doubt
that they tailed us. But for everything to come together, we
reached a compromise via intermediaries about where their
challenge would take place. We agreed upon the hour, pref-
erably the evening, the better to mobilize the audience that
we shared. The latter arrived before we did. They took seats
in the *buvette.* The dance floor was reserved for the event. We
proceeded with our preparations: knotting ties, waxing shoes,
oiling the moped motors, synchronizing our steps, and sprin-
kling ourselves with Mananas perfume. We spread out along
Independence Avenue. Outside, the frenzy reached fever pitch.

Every table in the *buvette* was occupied. We were applauded on the avenue. We were encouraged by enthusiastic gestures.

"When the time had come, we left the neighborhood for the site of the challenge in enemy territory. As I was the president, I put myself at the head of the procession . . ."

—m—

This monologue made Moki grow hoarse. We sensed a certain joy within him. The legend of the Aristocrats, for him, was a recital. He picked it up again every year with the same emotion, the same words. Many of us had heard it several times without doubting its veracity. The audience was with him. We could hear flies batting their wings and mating on half-filled glasses of beer.

"Where was I? Oh yes, we were in our adversary's neighborhood. We got ourselves ready in the *buvette* dressing room. I gave the guys their final instructions. Who would be the first to go out in public? On the dance floor, a voice raised the crowd to fever pitch with the microphone. We chanted slogans, recited the names of those who were the most influential trendsetters in Paris: Djo Balard, Docteur Limane, Mulé Mulé, L'Enfant Mystère, Anicet Pedro, Ibrahim Tabouret, and many others. Our names and those of our adversaries were announced. We decided that I would appear last; that was the president's perogative.

"The battle commenced. The public was ecstatic. At bottom, they were waiting only for the grand duel between the two opposing club presidents. At the end of the first battle, the Aristocrats returned to the lodge. So did our adversaries. The two presidents were called to the dance floor. I slowed my pace. I didn't want to be seen first. I feigned surprise. An Aristocrat in the crowd gave me a signal as to whether I should move ahead or dawdle, depending on my adversary's position. We met each other on the dance floor at the same time.

"My adversary stunned me by executing an acrobatic leap that left the spectators cheering hysterically. He was dressed in a black leather outfit with boots and a black buckskin helmet.

He smoked a fat cigar and turned his back on me—one way
to ignore me and make a fool of me. I moved calmly toward
the center of the dance floor. I was wearing a colonial helmet
and a long cassock that swept the ground when I moved. I
held a Bible in my right hand, and while my adversary had
his back turned to me, I read aloud in an intelligible voice
a passage from the Apocalypse of Saint John. The audience
was euphoric, swept away by my originality. I had outwitted
all predictions, arriving at the *buvette* with my cassock and
colonial helmet hidden in a large suitcase. I had been dressed
differently. We pulled a fast one on our adversaries. The president of the opposing club had fallen into the trap. When he
turned around, he took note of the gap I had created between
us. I was cheered. The crowd was on its feet for the first time.
They chanted my name. I decided to speed things up. I had
another trick up my sleeve. I took the Bible and handed it to
a young girl, while my competitor looked on in astonishment.
He didn't grasp what I was about to undertake. He stayed on
his feet, blinking nervously. His cigar was no longer lit. He
chewed it and spat. He sweated big drops of perspiration. I
suddenly took off my cassock in public, then turned it inside
out. And, like in a magic trick, another cassock appeared in
scotch plaid.

"In fact the outfit was reversible."

On that last note, Moki was applauded.

Dupond and Dupont retrieved the photo albums from the
tables. They kept a watchful eye to make sure that not a single
photograph was stolen by the audience or the girls. Apparently,
Moki had not accomplished his return through the past that
the audience believed in. He had not yet recounted his odys-
sey, Paris, which was, to their mind, a sacrilege. This second
part of his discussion took the form of an epic. The details that
he described in his discourse gave the audience an idea of the
adversities one had to overcome to find safe harbor.

"You know, a Parisian has to move. He can't stay idle. He
has to know Paris, the Métro, the suburban rail, the buses, the
streets, the avenues, the squares, the monuments: he can't

have difficulty with any of that. But there's an entire history behind us. Don't you see that well-lit side of the mountain, what's called *the south facing slope* in good French. Am I being pretentious to say that we're practically heroes?

"I had left the country by way of Angola after failing my *bac* in literature twice. It was pure adventure: a youth who takes a risk like that today is rare. My family was not aware of my plans. Indeed, back in those days, one presented parents with a *fait accompli*. What could they do for us? They couldn't help in any way—least of all financially, which is what we worried about. We came up with all sorts of plans. Departures were certainly rare, but failed attempts didn't count anymore. If a youth were missing from the neighborhood for a long time, it meant that he had gone to France. And then nobody was alarmed by that. On the contrary, the family was proud of it, especially when they received, a few months later, a photo of their son in winter clothing.

"Those days were a long time ago. I also disappeared one fine day from my parents' house to head to the Angola border. I had developed my plan. From that moment on, it was impossible for me to wait, all the more so since several of my friends had been successful in their adventures—Préfet, to cite but one, who was the first to leave by way of Angola. Before him, our daredevil predecessors, if I dare say so, took the maritime route from the port in Pointe-Noire, with all the risks that went along with that. First of all, they had to penetrate the maritime world. So they worked as warehousemen at the port for months. Later, when they had acclimated to that universe, they picked an opportune moment to infiltrate themselves in the hold, not caring whether the ship flew a French flag or not. That's how some of them found themselves in Portugal, in Greece, or even in Latin America, thinking that they were heading to France. As you can see, this was a dangerous route. And that's leaving aside that there was nothing to prevent them from suffering the worst duties a perverse mind could imagine or, for that matter, getting thrown overboard in the middle of the ocean.

"I was stuck in Angola for several months. My pockets were empty. Nothing to pay for a ticket to France. Nothing to eat. But moving closer to that country compelled me to carry out my plan. I wasn't alone in that Portuguese-speaking country. Lots of other daredevils hung around Luanda and took advantage of that available connection. All you needed was a little money in your pockets and France was within reach.

"I acted like them to pull myself up and hope to get to Paris one day. I sold salted fish, sole, dorade, and cakes in a big working-class market in Luanda. I pulled together a large sum of money, thanks to this business, which allowed me to bribe the guys at the airport. They lived off this trade and got the daredevils who offered the most on a plane after providing the necessary travel documents. And that's how I disembarked one morning at Roissy airport in Paris . . .

"I was met in France by my loyal friend Préfet. He didn't come to wait for me at the airport. I knew Paris before I even got on the plane for the first time in Luanda. All the Aristocrats knew Paris. As soon as I got off the airplane, I confidently took a taxi and told the driver which way to go. He was dumbfounded. To him, I was not a foreigner. I was home.

"I lived for more than a month with idiots who slept all day long and lined up at the family benefits office. Those were phony Parisians. Is that the way to get a pair of Westons?"

Someone coughed.

Moki served himself another glass of beer. Dupond and Dupont were chomping at the bit and waving their fists to remind their brother that he had another appointment and he had to leave right away. The Parisian calmed them down. His movements were measured.

The chauffeur was no longer waiting outside in the street. He was in the car, head lowered, getting some shut-eye, one leg hanging outside the car.

Moki got up, his jacket over his arm, and continued speaking, standing up: "I can't imagine another country like France. I don't see it. So it's an unpardonable sin not to go there. To go there means to accept from that moment on never living without France again.

"What I'm telling you is that all of this can't be improvised. You need ambition, talent, faith, and love for what you're doing . . . I'm going to leave you; I'll spare you the tales of my trips back to the country. You know them all. Are there any more questions?"

Nobody else asked a question.

The Parisian had officiated his annual mass. He would do it again next year. With the same audience and some newcomers. He would omit a detail here, add another anecdote there. Silence was the sign that the crowd was with him. People lowered their eyes. Especially the girls. They would listen to Moki for days on end. He drank his last swallow and opened his agenda to make appointments with each one of the girls. He proposed that they come to his house to see for themselves the latest trends in Parisian fashion. He left the *buvette,* made his way through the middle of the crowd, preceded by his brothers. The car was idling. The door was opened for him. The girls hugged him, touching him one by one as if seeking his benediction. The car pulled out. The Parisian waved a hand out the window. The vehicle moved away.

I remember. I was there . . .

SO WHAT WAS my place in this race of aficionados? Taking his place was not even a question. I calmly observed everything. I watched from the shadows. I was there. Not far away. Quite close. I waited for the courtesans to leave. When it was my turn, I went to talk to the Parisian. I was as much a fanatic as the neighborhood youth. I wanted to know everything about life in France. But especially Paris. France was neither Marseille, nor Lyon, and certainly not cities unknown to us like Pau, Aix, or Chambéry. France was Paris, there, in the north of the country . . .

This harsh verdict drove us to raise a hue and cry against compatriots who returned from French provinces. The provinces? We didn't want to hear anything about it. No, no, and no. We called compatriots who lived there "the Peasants." No neighborhood youth were infatuated with that lot. They were exactly the opposite of Parisians. The Peasant's younger brothers had better watch it. Better to have not been in France than to come back from a province. The clever Peasants traveled to Paris first, where they stayed a few weeks, long enough to get themselves photographed in front of the capital's historic monuments, to cause confusion, when the time was right, in the minds of the population back home.

Truth exploded. Information got around from mouth to ear. The real Parisians forewarned the locals. They advised us to distrust *false prophets* who would speak in their name.

We had to sort the wheat from the chaff. On this occasion, they drew the typical profile of a Peasant: a sourpuss, an austere doctoral student. He returns home from the sidelines of what's happening. A homecoming with no echo, or drum, or trumpet. We didn't even realize he was back. Nobody except his own family would visit him. He isn't elegant. He doesn't know what elegance is. He doesn't know how to knot a tie in a few seconds. He has very dark skin. He doesn't cut his hair regularly and wears a "bouki" tuft on his head. He's bearded, mustached. His brothers keep their distance from him. If his homecoming coincides with a Parisian's, we compare them. We confront them. We want them to meet each other. The Peasant has no regard for the Parisian. The latter changes his clothes three times a day. The other comes back home with three pairs of jeans and a few T-shirts. At the very least a tight-fitting jacket just in case he might have to go to a ministry to request a document for editing his thesis. The Peasant goes around on foot and even has the nerve to take public transportation with the natives. The Parisian couldn't do that. The Peasant is a loner. He melts easily into the crowd. He writes, scrawls every day. He doesn't go to *buvettes*. The girls don't run after him. They ignore him. They make fun of him in the street when he passes by. There's nothing to be done but resort to his childhood girlfriends or women, the *unhappy women who married beneath themselves.* These spare tires make concessions discreetly. They divulge nothing about this relationship. It all happens at night . . .

The Peasant eats manioc and foufou. He eats on the ground with his brothers. He plays ball in the streets in rags with a few *old-young.* He helps his parents do their shopping at the big market. We hear him complain that life is difficult in France. Liar! Lying all the time. He lies like he breathes. And vice versa. He's nothing but a sourpuss, a good-for-nothing. Nobody listens to him. Nonetheless, he insists. He pretends that it's not easy to make it in France. Especially not in Paris. He wouldn't want to live there for all the gold in the world. He says that even French people dread life in that city. A cubic

meter is not within the means of every pocketbook. Rents are
high. France? You're going to France? "Why?" he exclaims.
The streets aren't paved with gold. From the time we began
listening to him, this is all that he would say. So how do the
others do it, the Parisians?

The Peasant lies. He's a big liar. He won't change. His frustration is the same way. He likes it easy. He's always com-
plaining. Advising his emulators to think twice before going
to France if they've got nothing going there. Be careful, you'll
roll around Paris like lost balls. I know what I'm talking about;
don't go there if you have nothing to do there.

It's a timeworn refrain.

A refrain we pay no heed to. Thankfully, the Parisian is
there to tell us the contrary. To bring us light. To talk to us of
the City of Light. The Paris that we love. He's the one who tells
the truth: come to France, you'll see, they've got everything
there, you'll be overwhelmed, you won't believe your eyes,
the city is beautiful, there are lots of small jobs, don't waste
your time at home, age won't wait for you, come, come, there
are apartments, if you're easygoing, you'll receive benefits,
come, come, one day you will have the same Mercedes as
members of the government, don't listen to these Peasants,
they are exiled in the provinces, they're blind, forty-year-olds
who are still hanging out on school benches with lower-class
Whites who could be their grandsons. Don't listen to them,
those types, don't listen to them!

And that's how Moki spoke, too. Charles Moki . . .

I had been listening to him for a long time.

I could practically recite his stories down to the last comma.
I went to their house whenever I wanted. His brothers
couldn't stand in the way. We had gone to school together.
Moki thought well of me. If I climb a little further up the path
of my memories, this admiration was the spark that lit the fire.
Indeed, one day he made a statement that yanked me out of
my somnolence. He told me that I had the right kind of face,
like a true Parisian, and it was really too bad I couldn't take
advantage of it. There were those who would never have it

and those who always had it. The latter would end up leaving
one day or another. Moki said that. They were the words of
an evangelist.

The effect was immediate. My head swelled. I looked at
myself, proud as Artaban. I took care of that mug so it would
remain intact and true to the image of a Parisian. I cut my hair
Parisian-style, short, with a part down the middle. I learned
how to walk like Moki, that slender look and those practiced
gestures. But I was a realist: I was not a real Parisian. I had a
hard time acting. I was nothing but myself. The pilgrimage to
Mecca was my default setting. A Parisian, according to what
people say, is above all someone who has lived in Paris. If I had
the look of a Parisian, then duty called for me to discover that
world . . .

I had succumbed to the charm, the enchantment. I nur-
tured my reflection. I didn't dare speak directly to Moki or to
my father about it.

One day, I made the decision to take the plunge. How could
I talk about it? Where to begin? Of course, I had the right look
going for me. But would that be enough? Could I go to the
emigration office or a travel agency with an argument like
that? And what if Moki doled out the same compliments to
everyone? Lots of youth my age had the same look. But they
hadn't been seen boarding airplanes for Paris. They hung out
in the neighborhood, telling the girls that before long they
would have it made, that a face like that didn't belong anywhere except Paris. I felt the birth pangs of determination.
The wings of hope would carry me far. Very far away from the
heap of illusions that all of a sudden seemed realizable. My
reason for being in the country was called into question.

I felt useless, lost.

That's probably what made me rush ahead and speak to my
father about this. I should have been tactful. Start speaking in
generalities. Talk about France, its grandeur, its influence in
the world, then recite for him the detailed list of riches Moki
had brought back to his family since he had become a Parisian.
My father was not the type that allowed himself to be stroked

with flattery. He was not expansive. Discreet, a good provider for his family, he taught us, my sister and me, to be content with what we had instead of looking to see what our neighbors had on their plates.

He listened to me closely that day. He added nothing to what he took to be a passing fancy. His silence bespoke his inability to help me financially. But no option was foreclosed.

To my great surprise, he encouraged me. "If this is what you have decided, what do you want me to tell you? It's just that to go to France, there's a minor detail to iron out. It would be good to mend the holes in your pockets, unless you want to go there on foot, in which case, get going today to have a head start . . ."

For once, he spoke a little more. He recounted his youth. He had done everything for our happiness. When he met our mother, she was often sick. She had chronic stomachaches. She couldn't give birth. He didn't want to leave her like that. His conscience wouldn't have allowed that. He spent all of his savings earned as an office boy to have children. He went from hospital to hospital, from sorcerer to sorcerer, until fate allowed her to become pregnant. Alas, she had a stillborn child, which once again threw a veil of sadness on their home. They had to wait for years for me to come into the world, then two years later, the birth of my little sister—whose delivery nearly took our mother away. They tied her tubes; she couldn't have any more children . . .

My father had tears in his eyes. He justified never having built a proper house nor having installed a water pump. He was exhausted and certain that the Lord wouldn't allow it. He asked himself if it wasn't the Lord who had inspired me with the idea to go to France? He was convinced that this would be for the good of the family.

"I have always thought that you would leave one day. Far away. Far away from here. Far away from this misery. But I'm sorry, my son, with the pension I get, I can't help you. I'm not promising you anything. I'll go and try to speak with your uncle. He's a clerk, and perhaps he could loan me something."

He also promised to speak with my mother. She sold peanuts in the big market. Even if her contribution were modest, he concluded, *"it's the little streams that make big rivers."*

So he would speak to my mother about it. According to him, she wouldn't see anything wrong with this. Instead, she would be happy. I would bring honor to the family. He himself could walk down the street holding his head high. He would be respected by the population and would carry weight in the decisions of the village council where Moki's father now ruled like a blind monarch. He would get even with everyone who denounced his poverty. He would be merciless. He would run the taxis that I would send them.

That's how he talked to me that day.

Through tears we had rediscovered good humor. We laughed. We had no reason to simper anymore. No misfortune had befallen us. We had to laugh to bring me luck . . .

My father got ahead of me by revealing the plan to Moki's father, whom he waited for, impatiently, on the way out of a meeting of the village council.

He gave him a bottle of *red wine from France* to grease the skids. Flattered, the president of the council took the bottle, not without putting on airs to extend the homage my father paid him, thereby raising the stakes. Nonetheless, he assured my father that he would take care of this and that from this point forward, I must consider myself completely Parisian.

He would speak with his son . . .

A few days passed.

My father came home one evening, saddened.

He had the face of a man who had weathered a hurricane. His features were deeply creased, his head lowered. He avoided my eyes. I rushed to his side. He had aged. I had never seen him so affected. One would have thought that he was suffering internally and stoically covering up his pangs of suffering. I needed to know the cause of his troubles. I had some idea. Someone had let him down.

He took me by the hand; we walked away behind the house. He informed me that he had contacted Moki's father a second time. At first, although he had indicated that every-thing would be taken care of, now he says that it's too late to get the administrative paperwork underway. Moki only had a few days left in the country. There were a lot of papers to fill out to get a permit for a sojourn in France, and these take a lot of time. I was missing a lot of documents, including the housing certificate, without which no exit visa is issued.

I calmed my father, who thought that Moki had opposed my departure for France. In any case, I didn't have my ticket, even if my uncle had led us to believe, in his convoluted manner of speaking, that he was *"favorably disposed to contribute to this very courageous initiative, but it was still necessary to discuss, at least the basics, without however putting the entire construct in question."* My father grasped nothing and returned without understanding my uncle's position, as his prose had so clouded his clarity. As a condition of administrative work, my uncle was the victim of this high-falutin jargon. With words like that, someone could refuse to grant you a favor without you even realizing it, you were so taken in by the polite and musical formulations. This way, they could also treat you like tramps—and you would agree.

I explained to my father that we had put the cart before the horse. That we needed to go step-by-step, and that one didn't travel to France without certain formalities.

I even went to see the Parisian to talk to him about it.

I met Moki the next day.

He explained the impossible situation he found himself in. He seemed remorseful. I saw nothing but sincerity in him. I would get it in the future, he said. I had made a good decision. He congratulated me. He declared that when he returned to the country next year at the end of the dry season, I would fly back to Paris with him and that as soon as he arrived in France, he would provide me with a housing certificate so I could get my visa.

At the end of our meeting, joking around, he tossed out an expression that I now use for myself:

"It's another world over there, *Paris est un grand garçon / Paris is a big boy . . .*" Five months after he left, Moki wrote me a letter that reassured me. He asked me to start the process as soon as possible to obtain a tourist visa. *"We'll see when you get here how to prolong your stay; the important thing is that you get into France."* In due form, a housing certificate accompanied the note. There was nothing for me to do but wait for his return to hope that my uncle's prose would be more lucid.

Things clarified themselves on their own.

I didn't try to understand anymore. Like my uncle's surprising attitude. He turned up one morning. His car was parked in front of our house. He went to drop off his children at school. My father went to meet him, his arms wide open as if he were about to embrace an ancient baobab tree. I was embarrassed by this self-serving enthusiasm. The uncle still hadn't said anything, and we weren't protected from his verbal circumlocutions.

My father suggested that he accompany him behind the house to talk man to man. My uncle replied that he didn't have time and that he was already late to drive the kids to their school. He shook my father's hand vigorously.

"Banco!" he said.

"What Banco?" asked my father, nervously.

"For the little one's ticket. I'll pay for the whole thing, and we'll work things out between us later."

My father turned toward me, incredulous, and took me in his arms.

My uncle sped away and waved from the gate.

—∞—

The housing certificate in my possession brought me closer and closer to Paris. The doubters and other miscreants who poked fun at the futility of my travel plan suddenly took me seriously. This document was a lover. It had powers of attraction. People wanted to see it, palpate it, smell it. Many among us dreamed of getting one.

I lived in permanent terror of losing it. This anguish dwelled in my unconscious to the point that it tossed the landscape of my dreams upside down. My nights no longer passed without nightmares. The themes of these haunted dreams did not vary.

I dreamed that a big whirlwind swept through the neighborhood, taking only my document in its wake. In fact, I feared
that a lout would steal it away from me. My precautions rose
to the level of my anxiety: I kept this paper with me all the
time. It had become a substitute for my identity card. I read
it every second. I verified that it was really still there, in the
little black cardboard holder I had specially purchased just to
protect it.

The document was wrinkled as a result of too much han-
dling, showing it off, and wearing it around. It was soiled with
grease stains. Which almost cost me dearly because when I
went to submit it to the emigration office, the woman responsible for pulling together the files had a moment of doubt and
looked me over from head to foot, asked me to take a seat in
a cane chair facing her, and told me to wait. She roamed from
office to office, knocked on one door without success, opened
another without knocking, found nobody, climbed the stairs,
rushed back down the stairs all the way to her office, rummaged through a large dusty register with cockled pages, the
house reference, which in principle should provide information on everything and nothing, she furiously chomped on her
pencil, spit out bits of eraser on the table, made a few squiggles
in the overly scrawled margin of the register and put it back
to gather dust beneath an ancient piece of furniture that was
sagging under the weight of files that hadn't been put away
for a decade.

That was when a second woman, round as a barrel,
appeared. She seemed to turn white under her coat of armor,
seeing how the first woman barked in desperation around
her, shoving my housing certificate under her nose. This second woman was cool as a cucumber. A matter of proving, as
much to the first woman as to me, that she was the undisputed
authority in the house. She breathed saliva several times over
her myopic glasses, wiped them with the hem of her woven
jacket, and proceeded to inspect the document with an air
of distaste that aroused my fears. She pretended to cough, to
scratch her braided hair, and to ram back the silver wedding

ring even further on her chubby little finger. Then she put her elbows on the desk, exhaled deeply, lifted her glasses, put them back on, and looked me over summarily before concluding that the document was authentic . . .

After that, I had my passport and my visa. I could have died of relief. I was bursting with joy. I didn't listen to anyone else. I spoke out loud, me the shy one. I pushed aside the flatterers. Those Johnny-come-latelies who try to make you believe they're your friends. It was a friendship of convenience. I didn't deceive myself. I chased them all away. People didn't look at me in the same way anymore. I was no longer a native. I was a Parisian.

My father advised me to be extra vigilant. He believed in evil spirits. According to him, they could ambush me at night and take my passport off me while I slept, or worse, erase the annotations on my visa.

I protected myself against all that. I had gotten used to it. Under my pants, I hid my passport in my underwear. I slept with those pants and that underwear after checking that the evil spirits my father spoke of had not ripped off my visa . . .

Waiting for Moki's return was a heavy cross to bear for me. The nights were interminable. I slept quite late. I went dancing with friends. My father kept watch over my every move. He scolded me when I crept home at dawn on silent cat's feet.

It was at this time that I found myself mixed up in an incredible story, to say the least, one that remains etched in my memory. As was our custom, my father led me behind the house to have a talk with me. He scratched his beard in silence and had an uncertain gaze. That was his way of expressing puzzlement.

"I told you to always look out for yourself, to be vigilant— now look what's happened to us all!"

He spoke obliquely, not going into the heart of the matter, moralizing in a tone imbued with sadness and fatality. I held myself back from pressing him to get to the point. Not because I didn't know what lay in store for me but because he was touchy. Besides, I didn't want to precipitate my own suffering.

He was the type who was easily annoyed and wouldn't bring up the reason for his discontent until a problem put me squarely before my responsibilities and finally demanded his intervention. He waited for me in this roundabout way and then announced his optimal solution:

"You have behaved like a crocodile who plunges into the river to avoid getting wet in the rain on the bank . . ."

So far as I could remember, he had never hit us—my sister and me. He believed in the power of words. His anger and tirades were sufficiently convincing arguments to make us dread the worst.

What kind of mistake had I made to make him take me behind the house? I indicated my impatience. I cracked the knuckles of my fingers. I bit my nails and drew I don't know what with my foot on the ground. He said that he was not happy with what was being said in the neighborhood.

"Do you know Adeline?" he asked.

I took a while to answer. He took my silence as affirmation. He explained to me that a young girl named Adeline had come with her parents and presented herself at the house. She claimed to be pregnant by me. My shock amused him and made his feigned mask of anger more severe.

"Don't play games with me. I know this game. I'm your father and you must speak frankly with me. Yes or no?"

I complained mightily.

"I knew the girl," I replied to my father. "But she went out with most of the guys in the neighborhood. Her nickname was 'garbage can.' She chased after all the future Parisians. Yes, I'd had sexual relations with her. That was some thirteen or fourteen months ago. After that, I didn't see her anymore. I couldn't be the one responsible. No. Impossible." It was a plot. I was not going to let myself get nailed by that girl who didn't have a good reputation.

That was not my father's view.

"Stop acting like an idiot. That child will be yours, ours, because the young girl said so. She knows her body and who she sleeps with better than anyone. I couldn't care less what the infamous village says. Think of your mother, who can't bring more children into the world. Why do you want to deny your own blood, the blood that we have given you, the blood of my father, your grandfather, your mother, your grandmother? Faced with this situation, you should get out in front of it. I made a compromise with the girl's parents. We will avoid bringing this business before the village council. I acknowledged the pregnancy, and we will take care of the child even during your absence. The child will carry our family name. Adeline will come live with us until she gives birth . . ."

That's how I became the father of a child. A little boy. He was raised by my parents. They remained indifferent to the rumors and lies flying around the neighborhood. I wasn't so quick to adapt to paternity. I felt embarrassed when I looked the brat in the eye. I felt like I was cheating, lying to myself. Taking the place of a vile father. At least the mother of the child had preferred me by saying nothing about her condition to the real father. A hypothesis that held up, in my opinion. The baby's innocence fueled my permanent embarrassment, which paralyzed my joy for this little creature that, according to my mother, looked like me. All mothers are alike. They see resemblances everywhere, going as far back as a twelfth cousin.

Was he my son? Was I his father? What is a father? Is it the progenitor or rather the one who takes on the burden of blazing trails for the child, leveling the ground for his path to assure him the opportunity of building an existence? And what if the real father of the child lived just an alley away from our house?

I hadn't said another word to Adeline. She used my father as an intermediary to speak to me. Her kindness and the time she devoted to my parents earned her stock of incomparable respect, which I had to acknowledge. She helped my mother sell peanuts in the big market. My mother lavished attention on the one she had now taken as her own daughter. My sister rallied to their side. She accompanied Adeline to town for food shopping for the baby and to the clinic for his weigh-ins and care. I was isolated. I'd find them all together, chitchatting, laughing full-throated. I sulked in my corner, which did not change their behavior one iota. They imposed Adeline's presence on me indirectly. If I accidently happened to reply to her, it was to offer harsh words regarding her morals. I was having none of this child. In front of the family and Adeline, my mother asked me to take him in my arms and rock the baby.

Little by little my resistance softened. Monotony beat it down. My resentment withered. I was surprised to find myself talking with Adeline, the child snoozing on my legs . . .

Moki finally came back . . .

He had gained weight. Even more Parisian than ever. He had bleached his skin so much we could see his veins. He wore contacts. His eyes were blue. He smoked a pipe. He said it was the *bourgeois* look. I accompanied him everywhere he went. I had become a valet. Mute, I waited in the background while he talked with friends or young girls. I was beginning to get irritated with this situation. The Parisian was obsessive about leaving me behind. He introduced me when it was convenient to do so. He said that I was a future Parisian and that I was in training for the big day. At those times, my chest swelled. I imagined myself to be just like him already. In my head, I would top the priority list as soon as I was in Paris.

What would I do about the family?

First of all, send money to my father so he could pay back my uncle. Then demolish our house made of old boards and build a permanent home. A big one. A magnificent villa. Deep down, I dreamed of a villa more beautiful than Moki's. I would also buy cars. My parents would use them for business. My mother would stop humiliating herself behind a stall at the big market, selling peanuts, retail. She would devote herself solely to depositing the daily taxi receipts. She would give the car keys to the chauffeur every morning. I would also need a general store. Moki had never thought of that. This store would be managed by my father. My sister would be the cashier. I knew that they would include Adeline.

I wouldn't forget a water pump. Electricity, too. We lived with hurricane lamps and candles. We didn't do our home-work assignments because at night we didn't have light, no money to buy a candle or a liter of oil for the lamp.

We abandoned our studies—my sister in secondary school, me, in the first year of high school. My sister wanted to become a midwife. Me, I would have liked to study law. To be a judge or a lawyer. For that, you had to earn a baccalaureate, go to university in Brazzaville, more than five hundred kilometers from our home. To achieve that, it was advised that starting in high school, you read and reread, and buy the books—which were no longer provided as they had been in grade school by IPAM (Institute of Pedagogy for Africa and Madagascar). In primary school, we didn't read at home. Our memories were so receptive that we retained forever what the teacher said or wrote on the blackboard. I've never been able to understand that miracle. As you grow up, that capacity diminishes. The brain aroused and occupied with a multitude of discoveries demands exercise, training, and lasting endurance. Reading and reevaluating become imperative. We didn't have light. When we got it, the light was not supposed to be left on a long time in order to save oil for the days ahead. Turn them all off when going to sleep at seven o'clock in the evening.

This time we would have electricity, current, circuit break-ers, bulbs—we would have all of that. I made it a promise. Water would run like a torrent in the courtyard. And the neighborhood would come to our house to buy casks of water . . .

I calculated my success in comparison with Moki. He had already started and was well on his way toward reaching his goals. For me, everything lay ahead. I had to prove my capac-ity to succeed. To go like Moki, if not better. The disciple lives with this idea. Surpass his master. Set the bar even higher. I was ready for anything. I had made up my mind to knock myself out. To work in France twenty-four hours a day.

Like a negro . . .

The departure date had arrived.

We were going to get a flight toward the end of the dry season. It was the month of October. A Sunday . . .

Sunday, October 14th.

The day of rest demanded by the Lord. My parents were there. My mother dressed in a new outfit of multicolored cloth printed with a picture of the smiling president of the Republic, blessing children in a hospital deep in the bush.

My father, he was dressed in a West African grand boubou with sparkling embroidery on the chest and shoulders. He must have struggled to find those clothes. A week earlier, he scoured downtown Pointe-Noire and got my mother's outfit and his own on credit from a Lebanese guy he knew. An old friend. Despite their friendship, the shopkeeper expressed reservations. The favor being asked was, according to him, beyond my father's credit rating. One outfit, sure. Two, that was too much. My father convinced him that this was an exceptional circumstance: the departure of his first-born son, his only son, for France. For Paris.

His eyes sparkled with admiration. In a heavy accent, he exclaimed: "Paris? But we must celebrate this, my friend!"

He took my father to the back of the store. "Please, my friend, follow me."

They went into a dark room where the shopkeeper kept his stock of new deliveries. The strong odor of mothballs dissuaded termites and other pests of their ilk from launching an offensive on the Lebanese man's merchandise. The man was well prepared. On one shelf, an assortment of Fly-tox and other similar insecticides—his armada in the little war that he waged particularly against cockroaches overly inclined to deposit their progeny in the inside pockets of jackets.

My father and the shopkeeper were surrounded by clothing that the Lebanese pushed aside to create a passageway. He had turned on the light in the room and told my father to make himself at home.

"Choose whatever you like. Come back to me to sign the receipt after you've made your selection."

My father reappeared with two outfits. He had chosen one for my mother. That evening, they both tried on their outfits in front of the mirror.

The couple was ready . . .

My sister was dressed conservatively. A white T-shirt with a blue cloth tied in a knot around her waist. My uncle didn't give a damn about the occasion. He had been in France at the end of the 1950s for his studies. Back then, he recalled for us, to find a negro, you had to cover the city with a fine-toothed comb for an entire day or wait at the exit for workers from a Renault or Simca factory. He emphasized, however, that the country had changed since then. He wouldn't even recognize where he had lived.

My uncle was wearing an Adidas jogging outfit and flip-flops. He normally wore a suit. Not on Sundays. He didn't alter his habits.

My sister had loaned one of her dresses to Adeline. It was already stained. The baby had thrown up on her shoulder and was crying. Adeline was unable to keep him from screaming. The roar of airplanes taking off and landing must have scared him. The kid nervously pulled away the rubber pacifier that was put in his mouth to calm him down. My parents no longer held back their tears. Neither did my sister. Adeline feigned sobbing.

My father took my hand.

I was waiting for this. We left the lobby and went toward a quieter area of the airport. We were surrounded by tall dry grass. Butards, weary of flying high in the sky in dry season with its huge cumulonimbus clouds, practically shaved our heads and perched on nearby shrubbery. An airport security truck passed us. It jerked and coughed black fumes from a crooked exhaust pipe, eroded and beat up by ceaseless scraping against the airport tarmacs. The driver in a blue uniform waved his index finger at us. He wanted to tell us that we were in an unsafe area. That tall dry grass was an emergency landing strip. We didn't follow his instructions. We walked. We kept walking. The plane wasn't leaving until eight o'clock in the evening. We were plenty early. My father had wanted it that way, despite what Moki had told him.

"I've never taken a plane in my life," he said, "but I know that just like the train, it's the traveler who must wait, not the reverse . . ."

And so we were among the first at the airport. My uncle packed us into his car like a sardines in a can to get us there around four o'clock in the afternoon. We went through the neighborhood, then downtown Pointe-Noire. Friends waved as we went by. We had no heavy luggage to check in. That was the reason my father suggested that we go where it was nicer. We sat down on a grassy mound. The airport was on the other side, a little further away.

My father began his speech with generalities. He beat around the bush, cracked a few jokes about the neighborhood girls, about how they wiggled their butts whenever they saw me lately.

Suddenly he turned serious. He warned me to be careful in life. I saw where he was heading. Don't touch White men's women. He had heard from one of his friends, a cook who had lived in Europe, that a White man wouldn't hesitate to use a gun or a chainsaw over business about a woman, while we, in our country, could marry several women if we wanted to.

"Don't marry a White woman. They also told me that men who marry White women disown their families. Is that what you want? Think of your old mother, of your father, of your sister, and now this child you're leaving with us. If you get married, I have the right to come to your house whenever I want, without making an appointment. That's not how it is with women over there. I've been told that. In their homes, when they're in the middle of eating, instead of inviting an unexpected guest to the table, they give him a newspaper to read. No . . . not those women. They prepare food and count only the number of people that live under their roof. My mother and my grandmother have always cooked by count-ing on a surprise visit by a family member or a stranger. These are the values they passed on to us and that are part of us—my brothers and sisters, your uncles and your aunts. They should not be lost. Open the door for whoever knocks, whoever it may be, whether he does it for something to eat or to drink a glass of water. Food is nothing. We eat in the morning, we throw it out the next day, holding our noses because it smells so bad. Your conscience, your education, they don't stink. They are odorless. I don't know how it is, that White country. Be careful, keep your eyes open, and don't act until your conscience—not someone else's—guides you.

"Yes, it's easier to correct a mistake committed by error of your own conscience. These will be my final words, I, your father, who has nothing and envies nothing belonging to anyone . . ."

He took a look around us.

No one had wandered into this area. He rummaged in the pockets of his boubou and took out a dried palm leaf and a clump of earth wrapped in a scrap of paper.

"Of course you don't know where this red earth comes from . . ."

I shook my head "no" and gave him an imploring look for him to tell me where he had gotten it. He told me that it was earth from the grave of his mother, my grandmother. He told me to get down on my knees. I did so without hesitation. He held my head and chanted, eyes closed. Then he told me to lie down on the ground with my eyes closed.

I carried out his instructions.

He stepped over me three times and then asked me to get up. He embraced me with all his strength and I saw tears pour like a storm down his wrinkled cheeks . . .

Going back toward the airport, we encountered the airport security truck heading in the opposite direction. The driver stared at us through a spiral of smoke, and we heard the exhaust pipe grate along the pavement for a long time. We returned, my father and me, hand in hand, and suffered my mother's terse pique. She was worried that we had taken our time to talk about who knows what when we had had the chance to do that back at the house. My father calmed her

down with a severe look and asked if Moki and his parents had
arrived. My uncle, taciturn and a bit withdrawn, pointed his
head toward where the Parisian was weighing a heavy suitcase. He was there, not with his parents but with Dupond and
Dupont. Those two, with their infamous brashness, rubbed my
parents the wrong way more than a little when they blurted
out in unison that their father and mother were used to this
sort of travel and didn't trouble themselves with it anymore . . .

Night had fallen. We had to move on.

Moki and I were on the other side of the concourse. We had passed through security control at the airport. They made us wait in a glass-enclosed room where we had to undergo final verification of our papers before boarding. From this room, we could only wave from afar to those who had accompanied us. I had embraced my family beforehand. My mother was speechless, her throat choked with emotion. She imprisoned me in her arms as if she would never see me again. I looked at her, stared at her closely. I, too, had the feeling that I was seeing her for the last time. This is the feeling all sons have when they leave their parents. Fear of the distance, of growing old, torn apart by regret—these make up so much of the pain that gnaws at the guts of the person staying behind as well as the one who is leaving. That brave and devoted woman, my mother, was from that point on another woman to me. The separation gave me stomach cramps. My mother wouldn't let go of me. She offered no more words, leaving her tears to express the sadness she suffered. With my father, it was just a quick hug, while my mother kept an eye on him, still spiteful over our complicit jaunt in the fields around the airport.

My uncle vigorously shook my hand and gave me a pat on the shoulder. My sister smiled, but she had tears in her eyes. Adeline kept her eyes fixed on the ground. She didn't dare meet mine. In truth, I also avoided her gaze. I had taken the child in my arms to hug him. I did it for her as well. This released the tension among family members, who noticed my tacit act of recognition of the union between her and me . . .

Next to Moki I was a skinny reed. The delay weighed on me in that room. All I had was a little gym bag. There was almost nothing inside it. Two pair of pants, a shirt, a pair of black shoes, my toiletries, a photo of my family, of my son, and of Adeline. I was lightly dressed and in light slippers, despite the fact that Moki had warned me that autumn could be tough for someone who knew only a tropical climate . . .

Our identities checked out, and we boarded. My heart pounded. The dream was becoming reality. Moki and I were seated side by side. Out the porthole, I saw the country shrink and become nothing but a miniscule dot, sporadically illuminated.

Did Moki notice the hot tears that misted my eyes without my knowing why I was crying? Where did they come from? They must have come from inside me. They clung to their course, somewhere in my unconscious. Take-off had messed up everything. The idea of being ripped away; of being tossed from a known world to another yet unknown. All these thoughts precipitated the outpouring of these tears.

There I was. Me, the shadow of Moki.

We went through the clouds and penetrated chasms of sky. Deep darkness, monotone and mysterious, slowly swallowed us. The feeling that the airplane wasn't moving induced sleepiness that, unsuccessfully, I tried to evade so as not to disappoint Moki. Unfortunately, I could barely still listen to his voice. He spoke to me. Snatches of words. Names: Préfet, Benos, Soté . . . A place: rue du Moulin-Vert . . .

We would travel all night long, it seemed to me I heard it said. Paris would not appear until the first glint of dawn. That was what he told me.

I wasn't listening to him anymore . . .

PART TWO

Paris

It seems that the gates of hell
border those of heaven.
The great joiner designed them
in the same coarse wood.

—Abdellatif Laabi, *Le Spleen de Casablanca*

RUE DU MOULIN-VERT (14th arrondissement, Paris)
MARCEL BONAVENTURE
ERIC JOCELYN-GEORGE
CHÂTEAU-ROUGE (18th arrondissement, Paris)
THE REAL ESTATE AGENT
THE ITALIAN
CONFORAMA
THE WORKHORSE
PRÉFET
SEINE-SAINT-DENIS

I MUST REMEMBER THOSE DAYS.

It's a must.

I mustn't let myself be distracted by a single dark cloud of forgetfulness. Everything flows in the slowness of memory. The past is not just a worn-out shadow that walks behind us. It can get ahead of us, precede us, bifurcate, take another path and get lost somewhere. We must find it, lift it on our shoulders, and get it back on its feet.

I must remember.

As if it were yesterday. As if I were reliving those moments back then, with the candor of the *débarqué*. The eyelids finally open up on those days, on those nights.

Try harder.

Resist easy abandonment, abdication, and resignation. Somewhere the clarity of rebellious truth awaits me, truth that refuses to lie low . . .

I spent hours flagellating myself to punish these limbs, this head, these eyes, these ears that led my good judgment astray and abandoned me like cowards to my fate.

To flagellate myself wasn't a solution either. Tranquility does not reconquer the spirit until a man takes responsibility for his actions. I would simply like to find a passage, a way out of this abyss. I am not pleading for memory to help in order to beg for some sort of absolution. What was done is done now. All my thoughts are in motion, on their feet in Indian file.

What concerns me is to direct their march such that they are not derailed on the slope of regrets . . .

I must remember those days.

Those days so long ago. So near. Those days that brought me here. Me, Marcel Bonaventure. You heard me right. Marcel Bonaventure . . .

I say this name because over time I became accustomed to it, even though it isn't my name. In reality, I don't know who I am anymore. Here, one has an infinite ability to split oneself in two, to no longer be what one was in order to be what the others would like you to have been and even sometimes what they would like you to be. Of course, under the circumstances, they're right. One can't do otherwise. This is how one builds one's own fortress. I don't dare say one's own grave because I'm counting on getting out of here, no matter what happens.

Use another name.

Forget his name because that's necessary for the cause. Distance yourself from the ordinary world, the everyday world. Be on the margins of everything.

Me, Marcel Bonaventure, I vow and reavow that up until the day that I landed on French soil, that Monday, October 15th, at dawn, my name was still Massala-Massala. The same name repeated twice. In our dialect, that means: *those who remain, remain, those who stay will stay.* The name carried by my father, my grandfather, and my great-grandparents. I thought the name was eternal, immutable. I thought the name reflected the image of a past, of an existence, of a family history, of its conflicts, its rifts, its grandeur, its decadence, and its dishonor. Yes, I thought that the name was sacred. Not something to change like clothing to dress appropriately for any given party. A name like that is not taken without knowing where it came from and who else besides you carries the name.

But what is a name in our little world onto ourselves, here, far from our homeland? The name, a label on merchandise, a passport that opens borders, a permanent pass. The name is worth nothing.

The name carries no history whatsoever for us . . .

I am Marcel Bonaventure—that, I'll remember. No matter what becomes of me. I can't cross that name out of my memory anymore. I carry it like I carry the name Massala-Massala. I'm no longer just one person. I am several at the same time. Someone in the street says the name Marcel Bonaventure? I turn around. It has to do with having a split personality.

I don't even speak of the other name, Eric Jocelyn-George. No, I would rather not garble the intelligibility of my remembrance. It's confusing enough as it is without speaking of this third name: Eric Jocelyn-George. It's still me. Me, Massala-Massala. Every name has its own history. Every name is a time period, a fact of my existence.

Where are they, the ones from our milieu?

So where are they? I sound out the walls of silence. Why do I hear nothing but the echo of their voices? They all had wings to fly when the stone, thrown by a rowdy child, had fallen smack in the middle of the courtyard where we were arguing over a bread crumb, like birds. I wanted to fly away, too. I was nothing but a fledgling. You don't fly all of a sudden without running into a void, the force of gravity. You have to proceed by steps. Climb the walkway of patience. First, stretch out the wings, then flap them to catch the wind. Curl up the legs and leave the nest for the first flight. I was just a fledgling. I flew by mimicry.

So that's why I ended up here . . .

I had been living in Paris for a few months.

I was getting over my bewilderment. The shock of reality gnawed away at me. Moki, for better or worse, made an effort to console me, sensing that I was sinking into disillusionment. There was nothing more he could do. I was annoyed with him for not being more explicit about a certain number of things. About the essentials. I certainly wouldn't have made the same decision.

I guessed his sin was one of omission. A voluntary omission. The most serious there was. One that so closely brushes up against lies, hypocrisy, and cowardice that it takes a long time to absolve.

I didn't speak to him during those first weeks. Then not for a whole month. I closed in on myself. I built a wall between him, his people that would come and go, and me—immobile, taciturn, brooding over the bitter leaves of resentment that inflamed my lungs. He could tell I was vexed. He and the others had all noticed it. A kind of bitterness with a brackish reflux that came up in my throat when I thought about my surroundings. My silence unsettled them. As for Moki, he expected a more virulent reaction in response to the scene that confronted me. A reaction of revolt. He thought that I would demand an explanation. But no. Silence. Only silence. None of those types of questions. Why? . . . How is it that? . . . But where are the? . . .

None of those types of questions.

—ɯ—

Everything happened fast.

Naked reality. The impossibility of backing out. The obligation to integrate myself in the milieu. Time itself seemed stubborn, suspended on branches of disillusionment. Sleep. Always sleep. Moki's feigned sorrow, saying that he had done everything in his power for me to be in France. The rest was entirely up to me. And my will to succeed and to get out of this. He would pull a lot of strings for me. For now, I remained pensive, not knowing where to orient myself. I was hanging on Moki's willpower and, as I realized later, on the will of others in that milieu . . .

It wasn't so much the idleness that hacked me apart but the desire to write letters home. It's an urgent need in the minds of everyone who leaves a chapter of themselves thousands of kilometers away. From then on, words are the only connection. A letter in the mailbox is the good news of the day or, rather, the month when there are longer intervals between those missives, as time erodes desire . . .

I remember the story of the letter from Marie-Josée. It was that day I was seized by profound nostalgia. I felt this anguishing void, this desire to write home, to my parents, to a few friends, to give them news of me and to talk to them about our existence here. My mother's face appeared before me—very emotional, ravaged by my absence. My father's face, serene but brushed with well-disguised worry. The tearful laughter of my always carefree sister. I imagined that she was confident, sure of herself. Adeline had, in my thoughts, lowered her face. The child whimpered on her knees. My uncle was there with his sloppy clothes. Therefore, it had to be a Sunday. Otherwise, he would have been wearing a suit and necktie. The grass yellowed by sunsets of the dry season. Nostalgia made ramparts necessary. There is no escape from the call that rumbles from the underground of the soul like a stampeding herd of buffalo frightened by a brush fire. I had prepared several letters written in the ink of anger and exasperation. About a dozen. Our life in Paris was described in detail, without sugar coating. Names and places were referred to. Back home, they would know exactly what I was doing. Where I was living. In what condition. And with whom. What Moki was doing. What all the others were doing. They would know everything . . .

I had to write.

What compelled me to ask, at the last moment, what Moki thought? He insisted on opening the letters. He read them one after the other and declared that I was naïve, irresponsible, a poor hick.

"Who do you think you are? You're wasting your time;
they won't believe you back home. Those people back there
have never changed, and they won't take pity on the tears
you will have spilled. They love the dream. You hear me, the
dream. They are children. They go crazy for candy and don't
understand that to buy it, you need money that you get at
the cost of tremendous effort and sacrifice. Don't explain to
them that *Paris is a big boy*. Everything you write is of interest
to nobody but yourself, and you'll be the laughingstock of the
neighborhood . . .

I didn't send letters home anymore. I didn't send any news
about me. Like everyone else around me. This way, they said,
we manage the suspense back home. Back there, they have
to wonder what you have become. A good picture. A picture
of a *fighter*. A picture of a Parisian. If I wanted to write, the letter had to recount all the good things I thought about Paris.
Moki would correct me. He would never miss an opportunity
to squeeze in, here and there, a superlative more bombastic
than my own.

I laughed my head off skimming the sort of letter that
everybody copied over. A letter written to a girlfriend back
home. The letter hung from a wall in the room, right next to
the broken window. Who had edited it for the community's
delight and happiness? I didn't know. Those who copied it
changed only the first name of the addressee. The letter was
addressed to a certain Marie-Josée, sweetheart of the anonymous author. One look at how it was stained made clear that
we were all schooled in the art of making carbon copies. The
letter was clear and summed up our desire to perpetuate the
dream.

My dear Marie-Josée,

I'm writing to you, facing the Montparnasse Tower, which
I admire every morning from the bathroom in our magnificent apartment in the fourteenth arrondissement. Summer is
almost over in the most beautiful city in the world. We are
heading into autumn, and then we'll move on to admire the
white splendor of the snow in winter.

I have bought you lots of presents, clothing from the top designers from the rue Faubourg Saint-Honoré. I have also bought you a pair of Weston loafers. I would really like to send them to you, but I'm afraid of you having a shindig with my local adversaries, folks who don't even know how much a pair of Yoshi Yamamoto pants cost. As for me, I've got nothing left to prove. I am a Parisian with a capital "P."

I soared through the sky in an airplane throughout an entire night, and even had the chance to use the facilities as we glided over the country, an opportunity that isn't given to just anyone, certainly not to peasants. In other words, I fed the fish in our Atlantic Ocean. It's all only to marry you "for better." There will be no "for worse" with me. I give you my word as a Parisian. Count on me. I am preparing our future. I embrace you tenderly. I love you, my little Golden (that's what they call the apples that I like here) . . .

Your Parisian fiancé.

—ɯ—

I had opened my eyes to another world.

What did I see in front of me? Those night owls. Those confabs that went on and on. The murmurings on the mattresses. I had doubts about my presence. About this Paris. About Moki's Paris. About the other compatriots. About those who saw it like this and accommodated themselves to it.

What could I do?

It didn't take me long to learn how to live differently. Between the shock and Moki's attitude, I was split in two. The circle closed again behind me. Moki had two faces. He wore several masks. One mask for the country. Another for Paris. His confidence bowled me over. I could put up with it—I just had to refuse to answer him. His authority bothered me. An authority attained simply because he had been the first to have tread upon this land of dreams. He was in his world. It was up to me to find my place. A little place that suited me . . .

And our lair?

I couldn't believe it. I didn't want to believe it. Yet I lived there for several months. I rotted there. It had to be done. We lived there, Métro stop Alésia, on the eighth floor, in a maid's room in the fourteenth arrondissement, rue du Moulin-Vert. A skylight on the ceiling spread poor daylight. Just a little light that flickered all morning long before brightening the room, because it had to circumvent the peaks and red-tile roofs of neighboring buildings. No other opening. Nothing.

The surroundings were a jumble of dilapidated, mismatched, lifeless furniture. You rarely saw people leave. When, by chance, they were out, they picked up the pace, warily, went into the corner store run by an Arab, and then immediately came back to their building. Cars were parked down both sides of the street. They never seemed to move from there.

What struck me from the first day was the sign at the entrance of the front gate, which read that the building, our building, was under demolition. The number of the municipal by-law was written in red. Work was planned to build a school and kindergarten cafeteria. To quell my fears and astonishment, Moki repeated his turn of phrase, which I finally fully understood:

Paris is a big boy, he said. Yes, a big boy, all grown up now and vaccinated. Forget about Moki from the country. Don't ask yourself questions and content yourself with achieving the purpose that led you to come all the way here. To that end, all means will serve well. Mark my words, all means. You'll start by going out and learning to live like we do here. There's no other way to succeed than this. Think about it. What do you want me to say to you? Take the first plane back? You can do that; you already know what awaits you back home. Worse than shame, banishment . . . As for this building, put your fears on ice. I'm in control of the situation. That sign was put up ages ago. No one here has seen a single Caterpillar in front of the entrance. So consider yourself lucky that you don't pay rent; it's a good way to start saving. We'll show you the ropes to pick up money where it's lying around, without breaking a sweat. For now, I'll go see Préfet, my buddy, who'll make your papers as soon as your tourist visa expires. He's a good, down-to-earth guy, just wait and see. We are in a foreign land

here. The final judgment will be back home. They're waiting
for us back there; it's unthinkable to go home empty-handed.
Who would commit such a crime? Only hicks . . .

—ɯ—

We had no elevator to get all the way to the eighth floor.
The building was poorly lit and smelled of mildew. There were
no other occupants besides us.

We could hear everyone that climbed up and down from
inside our room. Friends of Moki's whom I didn't know. We
all slept there, nobody knew what anyone else did during the
day. His friends arrived very late at night, like felines, mas-
ters of the art of positioning their steps on the wood staircase
without making it creak. In the room, they whispered, popped
open Heinekens, ate roast chicken, and went to bed around
2:00 a.m. to get up at 5:00 a.m.

We would wake ourselves the next morning, piled together
like cadavers tied to some sort of mass grave. To sleep, you
had to put a superior intelligence to the test and do without
all those hindering positions, such as stretching out length-
wise or spreading your legs and hands. Space would cost you:
a sharp dig of an elbow or knee, as needed. Gesticulating
or farting while sleeping was to be kept to a minimum. We
were doubled over, some under the little plastic table, the
only furniture in the room, others in the corners. The concert of snores no longer bothered anyone. We didn't know
who snored. We all went to sleep on the floor using big wool
blankets. Moki, the *landlord* of the place, claimed that once
you bought a bed in a foreign country, you were done for. You
were totally screwed. You'd end up forgetting the road back
to our own country.

I wasn't able to count all the occupants in the room. They
weren't always the same. There were more than a dozen compatriots sleeping in that tiny room.

I slept all day long to contain my bitterness. Moki and his
friends quickly took to criticizing me for being as lazy as a snail
in its shell. They warned me that, at this rate, I would blow

my chance of returning home. They spelled out the rules of caution. Shut the door.

Don't sleep with a lit candle. Knock on the door with our secret code: one knock, then wait a few seconds, then two knocks, and then cough—just once.

This was not a world of indolence. Idleness was the first sin. It blocked all perspective. It distanced you from all your compatriots. One idle day and you'd be lectured all night long. Each morning, the day had to be a battle. It had to start very early and end late, with a reward at the end. Speed was the watchword. I had to wake myself up. We weren't in the countryside anymore. Here, we ate standing up, never closed more than one eye, and kept our ears open day and night. We were on the move, ceaselessly. We didn't talk a lot but said a great deal to each other in very little time. We never phoned each other—you never know.

Another world.

I acknowledged that they tolerated my inactivity at first. I had the excuse of not having a single document that gave me the right to work immediately and venture out in the street without fear of bumping into a police officer. My visa didn't allow me to stay in France for a long sojourn. It was a tourist visa, the same exact kind that allows you to visit a country, not set up shop there for good. I needed papers. Different papers, if I wanted to stay in France for a long time. Otherwise, I would be undocumented. I said nothing at all about this concern. As far as I was concerned, things would work out. Moki was there.

While waiting, when the compatriots went out on *business*, I stayed there, cloistered, studying the walls grimy with sweat. I opened the skylight to let the cold morning air in for a few moments, so the rancid odor that impregnated the room would vanish.

It was through that skylight that I was able to study the autumn sky in Paris. I was already looking there, in those dark, dense clouds, for hints of a promised return to the fold . . .

—∽—

Resigned, I convinced myself that it was necessary to move on. Just to be here was a big step. Who back home would know that I slept on the floor? Who back home would know that I lived in this building?

Moki was right. My jeremiads wouldn't be believed. The religion of the dream is anchored in the conscience of the country's youth. To shatter those beliefs is to expose oneself to the fate reserved for heretics. I also felt the need to maintain the dream. To cajole it. To live with it.

That's what I was going to do.

I decided to look at things differently.

My *joie de vivre* came galloping back. I started to smile again. I was asked to take care of the cooking until I could become active. I accepted.

I knew a little about how to prepare dishes from our homeland. I had watched my mother and my sister prepare food. I could work miracles.

I set myself to preparing national dishes. Why me? It was also the rule. Because I was the one whose memory was still fresh enough to remember that cuisine. I was the latest arrival. In our little world, the last one over was good for doing everything. The Parisian predecessors must be respected, whoever they may be. Obey them, consult them, and worship them endlessly. The last arrival was dubbed with the surname *débarqué.* Up until another *débarqué* arrived.

Kitchen duty allowed me to discover a place that would later become a decisive landmark in my existence: Château Rouge, the neighborhood located near Barbès, in the eighteenth arrondissement.

I went there to buy exotic ingredients from our country, from the African continent. It was a place that reminded me of the markets back home. Manioc leaves, tubers, and smoked fish made me feel at home. I forgot that I was in France. I walked from one end of the market to the other, in the hope of bumping into a face I knew. The place was swarming with people who were primarily foreigners. A true tower of Babel.

Small groups of Africans spoke in patois at the top of their lungs and burst out laughing in eruptions of festive happiness.

They tried on clothing and shoes in the cafés across the street. North Africans sold watches, handbags, and cassette tapes along a side street, keeping their eyes open and necks craned like cautious storks to guard against a possible round-up by the cops. Two streets ran parallel to the market, and down these streets older women plied their wares and dozed off despite the brouhaha of the area. Passersby had to slalom between several bowls of red yams from Côte d'Ivoire and crates of plantains from Bobo-Dioulasso.

In front of the entrance to the Château Rouge Métro station, a kiosk displayed the major newspapers from African and Arab Francophone countries. The front pages of these dailies, weeklies, and monthlies rivaled each other with portraits of heads of state. A few meters away, other Africans braved the cold—on their feet for hours already, wearing gloves, they distributed flyers hailing, in broken French, the supposedly magical powers of sorcerers from the African continent, all homonyms, practically to the last letter. We took flyers from hands forced on us. Gave them a cursory glance and then threw them on the ground after crumpling them. The street was brimming with these scraps of paper. The same phrases to lure the hopeless. Promises of cures for all maladies, including sterility, cancer, and, in passing, AIDS. Promises of bringing a wife back to the conjugal hearth, of success in entrance exams, casting spells upon the person one lusted for. A marabout even boasted of having obtained legal status for several clandestine immigrants after casting a spell on everyone who worked at the Bobigny police station.

People jostled each other at Château Rouge.

I blended into that heterogeneous mass of humanity. I bought manioc, foufou, peanut paste, maize. While I was shopping, a police car emerged from a side street. I also had to play cat and mouse with the forces of law and order. Stealthily disappear from the scene. Along with the illegal merchants or those without legitimate status to stay in France, we would disappear into the crowd. I looked to the left and to the right and hastened my steps until I got to the next street. When needed, I dove into a café and ordered a glass of Monaco to wait until the danger had passed.

The police left empty-handed.

It was usually just police officers on a routine patrol, whom we wrongly took for a premeditated trap set to catch people without papers . . .

—⁓—

In our room, I lit the little camping stove with the long, rusty legs that made everything placed on it tilt. I reestablished the center of gravity with a spoon. I prepared a big pot of salted fish with peanut paste and fine herbs. It was a main dish with soporific powers. We wanted to sleep deeply at night to gain weight. A Parisian was not puny. We made fun of the fact that it was not easy to feed oneself in Paris.

My dish was seasoned with semolina made according to our custom. I kneaded it. I made a dense dough with corn flour. The pot, uncovered, simmered on the hot plate. Everyone served themselves, paper plate in hand. I received compliments from the greedy. A good beer accompanied the meal.

All of the occupants, except me, kicked in money for the meal. They gave me the total collected in the evening, and I did the shopping the next morning. I was given a dispensation against making a financial contribution, not because I prepared the food, but because I still wasn't working. I didn't doubt that this was temporary and that when the time came, they wouldn't hesitate to ask me to pay . . .

We were sated. We belched heartily without excusing ourselves. The smokers filled the room with a cloud. Those who, despite these meals, didn't gain weight swallowed Periactin pills. With that, the results could be seen within a few weeks . . .

Moki put me on a pedestal in his milieu. That would completely change the course of my existence, especially the meeting with Préfet.

I found a variety of people with multiple faces. Complicated people I tried to grasp. They all juggled shadows and light.

The masks they wore during the day miraculously concealed their nocturnal behavior and obliterated any natural urge for self-reflection, which would torment ordinary mortals. They had a sixth sense, honed through experience, facts, and observations about the universe they found themselves in. Over time they learned how to pinpoint flaws in this society they were not part of and to penetrate a world that was closed to them. Rising to that occasion had taken some time. The time required. The time to get themselves settled. They came in first through the small door, very quietly. Then they progressively invaded the space and had finally left their marks and raised the pylons of their empire. There they ruled supreme. On the outskirts of society. They were unpredictable individuals, capable of the best and the worst. In a novel, they would be dressed modestly in the clothes of antiheroes.

The multitude of people who gravitated around Moki, despite their different areas of activity, maintained connections with each other. Their paths went in opposite directions, crossed each other, met up, and in the end converged. They were characterized by the same spirit. The same white-knuckled grip and the same fury to bust their way out . . .

He introduced me to most of these people. His friends. The most influential in our world. His *most trusted collaborators*, as he called them, haloed him with pride.

Their nicknames intrigued me. Crazy, but accurate, in a sense. And such nicknames! Each of them had a nickname that evoked their particular expertise.

I knew that in this milieu Moki called himself the Italian. Which never ceased to pull a full-throated laugh from my throat when we weren't out in the street. Everything had an explanation. There was a reason for his surname. It was the reflection of reality. Italian, because he went to Milan twice a month to buy clothing to resell to compatriots who were heading back to the home country for vacation.

When he came back from Italy, the room on Moulin-Vert was crammed with clothing. A mountain of clothes to sell. At night, a stream of buyers. Mass production of trousers. Pure wool. Virgin wool. Alpaca. Cotton. Polyester. Leather.

Suede. Linen suits. Ties. Shirts, still in their packaging, which he threw on the floor to count. Moki excelled in his trade. He had a good feel for clothes. Nobody had any doubt about it. His clients were fully confident that he could buy for them with his eyes closed. He often put their clear-sightedness to sleep. They bought because they knew his past. One of the old Aristocrats. One of the most elegant men of the times. One of the most famous Parisians in the country.

When he couldn't leave for Italy, he pulled a hoax on that naïve clientele. He assured us that he was going to Milan or Naples. He packed his suitcases, grabbed his leather jacket under his arm, and off he went. We knew that this was just for show. A decoy. He would stay in France. He would disappear for two or three days and make his purchases in Aulnay-sous-Bois or at La Varenne, places on the outskirts of Paris. He would sleep in a hotel in one of those towns to lend credence to his deception. He would come back one evening and resell this clothing for twice as much as it cost in the stores where he bought it . . .

—m—

I met Benos.

He was a short compatriot who had stayed in his shell for eighteen years in Paris without going back to the country even once. His coarse, tattered clothes were the telltale signs of his devotion to a business that ate up all his time. He wore the same baggy clothes. A shabby boubou outfit with a red turtleneck pullover inside. His Palladium loafers were threadbare, and his toes, with hard, blackened nails, stuck out. He could have been taken for a pygmy parachuted into the middle of the city. Stocky, his face was etched in keeping with the traditions of his tribe, the Teke from the south of Congo. He smelled like sweat and could not have known what a good shower was. He scratched his head. Very curly hair, dusted a reddish-brown and infested with sediment of disgusting dandruff. He was bright-eyed. He was someone to be reckoned with. His grubby appearance fooled those who didn't associate with him. He forthrightly proclaimed himself a businessman.

We dubbed him Conforama, just like the box store in France. Benos was the household appliance and hi-fi specialist. He immersed himself in an activity coveted by the majority of Parisians. He knew all about the latest technologies in hi-fi and household appliances and walked around with a big bag stuffed with catalogs. If someone ordered something from him, he would deliver the merchandise to their home the next day. No paperwork to be signed. Or even seen. Or known of. His favorite expression was: *"Short reckonings make long friends."* To the best of my knowledge, he never showed how he worked in broad daylight. Much less work with someone else who could have *stolen his intel*—those were his words—and jeopardized his business. He had to learn on his own. To teach his methods would be to give the business over to someone who one day would no longer be satisfied with his appetite for gains. Those who worked with him did as they were told. They were nothing more than intermediaries. They received, delivered, and deposited in Benos's name. Someone had to teach him the tricks of the trade. I learned that he got his start with Préfet, the man who Moki was keen to introduce me to and who, to hear the number of times that his name was mentioned every day, was the most sought after man in this milieu. I didn't meet him until after I had met Boulou, the real estate agent, and Soté, the workhorse.

—ᴍ—

Boulou was the real estate specialist and was aptly nicknamed "the real estate agent." As his nickname indicated, he worked in the world of property. He worked with compatriots with the names of bulldozers as their surnames. Their mission was to comb through the buildings in an arrondissement to find unoccupied apartments, offering financial compensation to the squatters. They were paid in proportion to the size of the accommodation they were squatting. The Bulldozers acted under the meticulous orders of Boulou, the real estate agent. A real estate agent like Boulou ruled in every arrondissement of Paris, and he jealously guarded his exclusive hold of his fiefdom.

The fourteenth arrondissement became Boulou's only two years ago. He made sacrifices to attain this exclusivity. Sometime before him, a Zairian—with shoulders as wide as an armoire and who could bludgeon someone with his fists—was enthroned there. The latter was the type who would drown his adversary in the Seine as a sick joke. Having embarked for France in a ship's hold, the Zairian hoped to pursue a career as a professional boxer in Europe. He was sidetracked from his ambitions by worship of alcohol and dope. He ran with a gang from the Les Halles neighborhood and was implicated in several robberies, and always managed to extricate himself. Rumor had it that he trained to be a professional security guard, a dog trainer, and that he worked as a bouncer in several nightclubs in Paris, where he threw as many punches as he wanted at people who tried to get in without meeting the dress code or without knowing the password. His reputation as an implacable tough guy and colossus had been established. It was said that he had gone so far as to devour, all by himself, a barbecued sheep that his North African friends prepared for him at Château Rouge, in thanks for the empty lodgings he had given them as a squat.

Boulou had worked with this Zairian. Let's just say that this apprenticeship was no cakewalk. He watched the Zairian work. He learned his secrets. He probed everything he knew. He got his jokes. He jotted them down in his notebook. He went to the confabs with the former dog trainer and his clients. He learned, little by little, how to negotiate a price, how to change locks, install electricity, gas, water, and a telephone line in a house that he didn't own.

He was punched out by the Zairian when he messed up. He put up with it. He hoped to one day get hold of maybe a quarter of the fiefdom. He didn't get too close to the fanatic when the latter spoke to him; you couldn't see his jabs and uppercuts coming. You found yourself suddenly on the floor, with an open cut on the eyebrow, bleeding.

Moreover, he was not surprised when the Zairian told him that he was giving up the fourteenth arrondissement for the quieter neighborhood of Champigny, in Val-de-Marne. The

strongman, Goliath, drew back and nestled into an anticipated retirement in the suburbs. The Zairian set the price of
the arrondissement at thirty thousand French francs.

"It's an insider's price for a friend; take it or leave it. I've got
a compatriot of yours who has offered me forty-five thousand
francs . . ."

Boulou raised that sum by breaking his piggybank and solic-
iting help from Préfet and Conforama.

The deal went down right away. Boulou had become the
new master of property in the fourteenth arrondissement. He
applied everything he had learned. First of all, always wear
a suit to impress the clientele; act serious. Shake a bunch of
keys. Look at your watch all the time. Go around in a small
car. Speak in French and not in African languages. Carry a cell
phone. Carry a briefcase full of files . . .

He was well aware that to spot an empty apartment required
sacrifices and considerable talent. You had to fight your way,
even in your own neighborhood. He hired the Bulldozers for
that work. They discreetly penetrated every building in his
fiefdom. If they didn't know the code to get into the building,
they patiently waited out front for hours on end. A renter
would eventually come in or go out. They rushed in.

Once they were well inside the building, they got to work
with used Métro tickets they had picked up from the stations.
These scraps of paper proved to have unimaginable uses. They
stuck them in keyholes and took off. They came back to those
places thirty days later. If the tickets had been moved, the
apartment was certainly occupied or visited regularly. If not,
they waited another two months, after which they declared
the apartment unoccupied—three months being the limit for
someone to come back from vacation, if the occupant had
really taken any vacation.

The real estate agent Boulou then proceeded to *sell* the
apartment. The eligible squatters were already on the waiting
list, just like the housing allocations through the social welfare
office. The families were landlords. The payment was counted
in cash. See nothing, know nothing was the rule of the milieu.

The clients occupied the premises and put up with the uncertainty of the possible return of the legitimate occupant. That's where Boulou put the experience he had gained with Goliath to work. In order to hold on to his clients, he promised them a four-month warranty, so that if the legitimate inhabitant reappeared within the first few months after the squatter had moved in, then 60 percent of his deposit would be refunded. The remaining 40 percent covered the costs incurred by Boulou for drawing up a false rental contract—it was Préfet who took care of that—and the Bulldozers' work. The latter broke down the door, changed the lock, repainted the walls, and installed a mailbox in the client's name . . .

—m—

Soté the workhorse was someone who you felt was treacherous from your very first contact. He accepted the image of himself as a despicable man and worked at it to the point of caricature. Maybe he didn't want to run with a crowd that was not of his choosing, and he distrusted every foreign face.

For me, he was the most unpleasant of all of them. No humanity. No heart. Profit dilated his mauve pupils. He never said a word about his activities. Tall, with bushy eyebrows like circumflexes, a face ravaged by pus pockets of pimples that he picked at in front of the person he was speaking to, Soté didn't take himself for a nobody. He was aware that he was a force to be reckoned with as much as Benos alias Conforama, Boulou the real estate agent, or Préfet, the man whose name was on everyone's lips. They needed his services. It was that dependence that made him so self-important.

His contact with me was limited to an exchange of inquisitive glances. I understood that he figured there was nothing he could get from me. In that case, he threw you aside like a sock with holes in it. He ignored you. I felt third-rate, worthless in his eyes. In any case, I recognized that he was an effective operator. His work was the work of a real professional. People said that he worked without leaving so much as a trace, without running into trouble, and that he worked with disconcerting ease. A specialist in mail boxes, he made his way around remote provinces where certain banks still trusted the mail with their clients' checkbooks.

The workhorse and two engineers traveled with their toolboxes. The engineers picked the spots and shadowed the postman before the workhorse personally intervened. They rented a hotel room and worked for a week, sorting the mail in the mailboxes with a fine-toothed comb. When they returned to Paris, the fruits of their harvest were snatched on the market. Half the checkbooks were reserved for Préfet, who acquired them for his own purposes . . .

When I met Préfet for the first time, I was enthralled. I had heard his name mentioned so often here and there, I was expecting an imposing, powerful, and charismatic figure.

The man who stood in front of me was the opposite of all that. Despite the smell of alcohol that told me he readily raised his elbow, something inside me whispered that this man and I would one day be tied together as if we were married, for better and for worse.

His personality radiated humanity and generosity, which was rare in our circle. Unless that was just an impression. The mask, in this milieu, surprised nobody. Préfet was short. As short as Benos. His hair was cut short. His cheeks and chin were mottled red with scabies. I found it difficult to look at him. His eyes rolled around non-stop in their sockets before settling on someone. He glanced at his watch. His time was precious.

Nobody really knew his name.

Maybe Moki. We only called him by this surname without knowing where he came from: Préfet. Many pronounced this nickname in Paris yet had never physically encountered the person.

Convinced that elegance was the key to the universe, he wore luxury clothes with designer labels: crocodile Weston shoes. He took pride in having a whole collection of these shoes. He had the means. He bought them on the Champs Elysées in that famous store where his face was no longer unknown. It seemed like the salespeople bent over backward from the moment he walked through the door. He didn't try on shoes in the main room. When he arrived, the sales help, dressed in penguin suits, smiled solicitously and escorted him to the second floor where Préfet could take his time indulging his fancies, ordering unique colors, for example.

He and Moki were old friends. Since the renowned epoch of the Aristocrats. Préfet had been Moki's assistant. Of all the youth from those days, he was the first to come to France. He loved telling how he had seen all his compatriots invade Paris and that he had arrived in this country when Pompidou had just come to power. He christened himself "the Savior of all." Which was the truth. For the most part, the Parisians owed their sojourn in France to him.

To whom had he not sold residency papers? He didn't live by that alone. He knew the ropes. He had help from *the white pipeline* that provided blank documents. All he had to do was fill them out by referring to an authentic document. He had changed identities several times himself. At least twenty times. He was never the same. A chameleon. When he was caught with his hand in the cookie jar and jailed—which had only happened twice, in itself a remarkable feat here—he served his time, got out, and wove himself a new identity. He was reborn from his ashes.

He said that he was the most sought after Parisian by the French police. He swore that he would never go to prison again, that he had not a sixth sense but an infallible seventh sense, that he knew some policemen, that he had influence, that the day they'd catch him there would be no tomorrow. Word was in the milieu that several Parisians ended up in prison because of him. They were mistaken for Préfet; meanwhile, he was running around town . . .

Of all of us, he was the one who *declared* the most income. He earned at least fifteen thousand Francs per week. He asked the incredulous to multiply that amount times four to estimate his monthly revenue. Paradoxically, he was the Parisian who had no *business* at all back in the home country. Not even a house. Indeed, he hadn't returned to the fold for a good twenty years. His family—his mother, his brothers and sisters, since his father passed away—wallowed in extreme misery, with no news of him. He was cut off from the reality of the country of his birth and childhood. Did he realize that when he left the country there were only three paved arteries: rue des Trois-Martyrs, rue Félix-Eboué, and then later, avenue de l'Indépendance in Pointe-Noire?

In those days, television didn't exist back home. We were a long way from imagining that life could be possible in that little box, which would repeat, without understanding what it blathered, words from poor images closed inside it, because its owner would press a button. Just one radio station, the State and the Party station, broadcast and rebroadcast the president's live speeches, the yammer of government sycophants, and a few death notices. Did he also realize that to take the plane, we first had to take a truck ride for hours through the deep bush, cross the border with Angola where bullets from belligerents crackled nonstop in a fratricidal war between that government's forces and the rebels led by Jonas Savimbi? That afterwards, we waited days, sometimes months, before seeing a plane land or take off?

It was a bygone era.

Préfet would have been surprised, arriving back in the country, to see downtown Pointe-Noire, the swanky neighborhood, and all along the wild coast where five star hotels sprang up: Novotel, Méridien, and PLM. He would have been astounded to find apples, strawberries, camembert, Bordeaux and Beaujolais, and butter croissants sold at Printania. He would also have been greatly stunned because now we have several airports more or less all over the country and asphalt roads in some large towns like Tié-Tié, OCH, and the Rex neighborhood.

Did Préfet know this?

He had voluntarily turned his back on the country. After the death of his father, we remember that to everyone's great surprise, he didn't come back, choosing to send a sumptuous zinc coffin and a white suit for the deceased. He admitted that he would not be able to accustom himself to life back there anymore. Was it for all of these reasons that he had become an unrepentant alcoholic? That was practically a form of punishment, a curse, imminent justice. How did he summon such a clear head to make his forgeries with the precision of a watchmaker?

Another fact astounded me.

I didn't believe it: despite his shadowy high earnings, Préfet was reputed to be without a permanent address in Paris.

At bottom, this was self-explanatory, if you thought about it for a moment. For him, this was a strategy. He didn't want to have a home of his own, the better to shake the police who hounded him.

Préfet could be the nicest one in our milieu. I sensed that from the start. He was ready to give his help to anyone who asked for it. A friend. That's why Moki introduced us.

Shaking hands with us, I felt electricity surge through my body. He was smiling. They had talked beforehand. He sized me up as if to assure himself that I had the stature of the man he was looking for. Yes, he had to look for someone. He didn't stop nodding in agreement, in complicity with his friend from youth. I made a good impression on him. There was no doubt about it. I could sense that by all the nodding of his head.

Moki had said to him: "Take care of the *débarqué,* give him a specialty because he's not doing anything right now. I promised to introduce him to you. Voilà, it's done. You're his godfather."

They burst out laughing.

They discussed legalizing my sojourn. By that time, my visa had expired. Several weeks earlier. So I didn't have the right to stay in France any longer. I was extra careful every time I went to the Château-Rouge market.

I couldn't go to the police station to ask for a residency permit. There was no justification for my presence in France. You had to have a reason. School, work, or family ties. I wasn't a student. I didn't have any work. My entire family was back in the country, and I wasn't married here.

—〜〜—

As Moki had planned, the task of establishing my legality was entrusted to Préfet, who took it as an honor to take care of this. Still, it took him two weeks. His famous *white pipeline* became increasingly reticent. Business wasn't working like it had in the past. The laws changed from one government to the next. One government would come to power and reopen the whole debate on the prior government's legislation. When the other returned to power, the business would be turned upside down again. And so on and so on. In the end, the police precincts, swept along in a ceaseless legislative waltz, no longer knew which procedure to follow. In the morning, they determined your status was legal, and in the afternoon, with their fists on the table, laws, presidential decrees, and official newspapers in hand, they solemnly denied it and gave you an appointment in forty-five days and a list of documents to provide, some of which were in the possession of your great-grandmother or one of your mother's three former husbands. A little more, and they would have demanded that applicants provide their baptismal certificates and bicycle permits.

This is how those who had residency permits found themselves *sans-papiers*—undocumented—sandwiched between complex and draconian laws. This theme was used as a political football to win a vote or two from intolerant French people. The abandoned and undocumented horde was considered a pressure on French society. Foreigners in France, they would be equally foreign in their own countries. After all, one can't just go back, impulsively, after an absence, which in some instances had lasted more than thirty years . . .

Préfet was a shrewd person.

He had changed his connections. Otherwise, he was heading straight to unemployment without compensation. He had tossed his friends aside. He had penetrated the Antillean world to such a degree that he spoke the creole of Martinique and Guadeloupe fluently. His summer visits to Guadeloupe and Martinique might have happened for a reason. Guadeloupe had particularly left its mark on him. He said he felt at home there. Old people who resembled our own. Tropical landscapes, that sea, like the Atlantic Ocean along the south of Congo. A municipality with the same name of the city where he was born, Pointe-Noire.

Préfet had quickly realized that he could work differently. Get in contact with his friends overseas. Some already worked with him then. Others were interested in easy money, without declaring taxes. They sold him their identity cards for a price that left no room for duplicity. Préfet bought the cards; the sellers made arrangements to later initiate the procedures to declare a lost card and then disappeared from Paris for a while. They knew that their administrative existence would be split with another person whom they should not encounter. If they ran into each other some day, they had to swear on the honor of their mother and father that they did not know this person who had *usurped* their identity. Which was true, because they hadn't established a relationship with anyone except the intermediary: Préfet . . .

This was one of Préfet's many tracks.

I remember that he proceeded differently with me. He had bought a blank birth certificate that came from a French overseas ministry. He filled it out with a name that wasn't mine, signed it, and put a seal on it with the tools of his trade, and we presented ourselves one morning at the town hall on the pretext that my French identity card had been lost. Préfet explained everything to me before going into those places that turned my limbs to ice. He waited for me outside. An affable employee, dynamic, so agile that she must have walked on her tiptoes, saw me, disappeared for a few minutes, came back, had me sign a pink paper, and handed me, with a toothy smile, the form to declare a lost card. I signed with such angst that my hand was sweating.

I walked out of there with the document in my pocket. With this declaration, Préfet and I returned to our local police . . .

I had a false birth certificate and a genuine declaration of a lost identity card. In less than one week, I had become a French citizen like any other, since they sent me an identity card in good time. My new name and surname was Marcel Bonaventure. I was born in Saint-Claude in Guadeloupe, a country I knew nothing about and couldn't locate on a world map. Préfet, having visited there, indulged me with tales of Soufrière, the famous volcano on Guadeloupe, in such a way that I could conjure a very clear picture of it myself without having seen it.

Of course, the name Marcel Bonaventure really did exist in the French territory of which I had become a national. Préfet kept silent about my Antillean double, who surely was out and about in Paris. This legalization was to lead me, without my even realizing it, into a vicious and irreversible circle.

With this, Préfet would at last reveal himself and appear to be just what he had always been . . .

I became clear-headed again. Several questions gnawed at my mind. They all came back to just one worry: why had Préfet been so diligent about me? I couldn't lay out anything to pay him back for this. All these procedures were onerous and cost tens of thousands. Although he liked to be Santa Claus, it was still necessary to live. He refused to discuss money with me right away. His thoughts must have come to light very quickly during the conversation we had on the way out of the police station where we had gone to retrieve my identity card.

"You'll simply do me a favor," he said.

"What kind of favor?" I asked.

"Work with me for a few months. That was the deal Moki and I made about you . . ."

"What deal? Work?"

"Yes, unless you've got another way to cover the costs that I've incurred for your papers," he said, while rolling his eyes around in his head. "These papers cost an arm and a leg. Usually I'm paid twenty to thirty thousand francs in advance, depending on the case. I agreed to proceed differently with you because Moki is one of my best buddies. So are you coming to work with me or not?"

I was no longer facing the Préfet that Moki had introduced me to. He was terse and spoke seriously.

In this world, nothing was done for nothing. I had no doubt about that. I had forgotten that too quickly. He wasn't joking. He was looking at his watch.

"It's a tiny job, no trouble at all. A job for rookies. The day after tomorrow is the end of the month, an appropriate date for this. You've got to be very early, six o'clock in the morning, OK?"

I agreed, in spite of myself. He and Moki had decided every-thing. For Préfet, my opinion was an afterthought. If I said no, what would I do instead? He was capable of taking back my identity card and tearing it up. Whether I wanted to or not, I had to reimburse him for what he had just done for me.

"For starters, you must get rid of this *débarqué* outfit. I'll bring you a suit the day after tomorrow, for which you will reimburse me, of course. I'm not the only one who will make a profit in this business; you'll see the results, and I am certain that you will beg me to do it again next month."

—☡—

For the moment, I had all my papers.

Yes, but I was haunted by doubt. I hadn't started working with Préfet yet. In two days, he would come pull the wool blankets off me in our room on Moulin-Vert to lead me who knows where. I questioned myself all night long about what sort of work I would be doing alongside him. I didn't see it. *A job for rookies.* The words came back to me.

The duplicity of people within our milieu intrigued me. Préfet, at first glance less charismatic, in fact had an authoritarian character buried inside him. An obsession they all shared to say nothing beforehand. To let the situation unfold.

I was in some sort of net. I adopted the same attitude: accept things as common sense.

Deep down, I had no doubt that he had thrown me a lifesaver. It was just that I had to be more careful. To know where my feet were going. My father's words came back to me like a deep echo from a cave. His words that he had murmured when we were sitting on the grassy mound at the airport: "*Be careful, keep your eyes open, and don't act until your conscience—not someone else's—guides you. Yes, it's easier to correct a mistake committed by error of your own conscience. These will be my final words, I, your father, who has nothing and envies nothing belonging to anyone . . .*"

I had a conversation with Moki in the evening about this rendezvous set for two days later. Of course, he was the one behind this. He played down the situation and assured me that this was the same path everyone had taken. He cited the names of my predecessors who had gone on to fly with their own wings since then. For me, this was the only emergency exit. He explained to me that with the kind of papers I had, it would be better not to sign up with the national employment agency to look for any kind of job whatsoever. These identity cards were meant to facilitate my movement around the area and not to disturb the siesta of an already jammed administration, which would suddenly rub its eyes at the sight of one letter spaced too far apart from another, knit its brows, and quickly crosscheck through the traditional channels between official bodies. Then I would be asked a lot of questions. When did you become French? And your parents, do they live here or in Guadeloupe? What is your father's profession? Your mother's? What is your social security number? Do you have a case number from the office for family welfare? Do you have subsidized housing? Where did you work previously? What is the name of your first employer? Could you provide us with proof of residency? A gas or electric bill, or a France-Télécom phone bill? And what about your tax return?

Then an accumulation of too many lies would petrify my tongue until I confessed . . .

I had to watch Préfet work, and one day I, too, would do it on my own. Don't let him out of your sight. Follow his movements down to the smallest detail. Obey him, and don't do anything except what he tells you to do. Don't ask him any questions. He won't answer. He will have drunk half a bottle of whisky to *see the situation clearly* and won't hear anything else you say to him. I would have to keep my mouth shut, and that's the end of it.

"The trouble with rookies," Moki said that evening, "is that you want to know everything before making a move. You have to go to work to earn something. It's a job. A real job, like any other. There is no shame or scruples involved. Why blush about this? Who said that money smells? I do this once every four months, this job, to pad my wallet when my clothing trade slows down a bit."

"Take a good look at my hands. Are they dirty? Cash that falls from the sky just like that is a good thing; it gives you

wings. You, you rookies, don't see anything except the con-
crete achievements we established back home. You don't make
an omelet without breaking eggs. Our sweat is not visible to
the naked eye like a warehouseman's. It's called *risk* because
it's well known that he who risks nothing has nothing. Every
job done by man has its explanation and maybe even its justification in a certain time and place. It's because I've also been
the victim of my own dream, this blue-white-red dream, that
today I don't allow myself not to take advantage of circumstances that fall right in front of my feet. I bend down and I
gather, that's all.

"I'm not a moralizer. I'm happy just to make my life and
my family's life the least miserable possible back home. You'll
achieve the same thing from here on out if you know how to
take advantage of the opportunities you're offered—I would
say on a silver platter—such as the one the day after tomorrow
with Préfet.

"What will you buy with the first French Francs you get
your hands on? I've seen everything here. Guys that went
running the next morning to a garage to get themselves a
set of wheels with their first earnings. Others who slept in a
five star hotel. And still others who went to Strasbourg-Saint-
Denis to grab a prostitute with big breasts and an ass like a
brood mare. I figure you'll go for that last form of rejoice . . ."

I SLEPT BADLY on the night before the rendezvous.

I had a stiff neck. I felt the contraction of my neck muscles when moving my head.

The room had emptied out of its occupants very early, as usual. Moki had gone to Milan. That's what he had led me to believe at the end of our tête-à-tête.

The air blew cold above the skylight. If the night always inhabited the sky, a few car horns outside announced that another new day was already up . . .

—ﾠﾠﾠ—

I heard someone knock at the door.

Someone from our milieu because he had honored the secret code. There was no need for me to look through the peephole. I thought it was Préfet.

I opened.

He didn't come in.

He remained planted in front of the door. He trembled from cold; the building wasn't heated. In his right hand he held a full plastic bag. He gave it to me by tossing it on the floor.

I discovered my work uniform. A grey suit, a sky blue shirt, a burgundy tie, and black loafers. He went down to wait for me on the ground floor while I got dressed.

Before going out, I couldn't keep myself from taking one last look in the broken mirror hanging on the wall. The mirror reflected a dismembered and fragmented image. One big eye. Two mouths. Superimposed teeth. Four arched eyebrows. Three nasal cavities. What difference did it make? I didn't know who I was anymore. Nor where to find the true reflection of things . . .

In lowering my gaze, I noticed my first photo in Paris, next to the Marie-Josée form letter. I was wide-eyed like an enchanted child. I didn't like that photo. Still, I kept it. It was my real face.

I was about to look away. I hesitated. Without thinking, I pulled the picture off the wall and slipped it into the inside pocket of my jacket.

I hadn't forgotten anything.

Yes, the clump of earth my father had given me. The earth from my grandmother's grave. Putting it in a pocket of my overcoat would protect me. I had hidden it in a corner of the room, under the rug. I dug it up. I brought it up to my nose.

The country was there . . .

At last, I could leave and close the door.

The key, I would put it under the doormat. I had no idea what time I would be back. If we had gotten up early, it was to go all day long . . .

—∞—

Préfet was in his Sunday best.

He had lit a cigarette. He rolled his red eyes, misted by smoke. He smelled of alcohol. He informed me that we had to go down the rue Pernety and take the number four Métro line all the way to the end, to Porte d'Orléans.

I waited for his instructions.

We got on the Métro at Pernety station and got off at Montparnasse. We took the long moving walkway to get to the platform to change trains. That's where he reluctantly muttered a few words without taking the cigarette out of his mouth.

"It's mathematical," he said.

"Mathematical?" I replied, as rapidly as his enigmatic words, while letting a few hurried people pass in front of me.

"Yes, think about it, Marcel . . ."

This name bothered me. Préfet knew his craft. He had already assimilated it. He struggled to nail me. The gyration of his eyes became epileptic. He was going to collapse, yet he fought back, grabbing the rubber handrails of the moving walkway. How could we work under these conditions?

"I said it was mathematical."

"That's indeed what I had heard, but it's not clear to me . . ."

"I'm getting there, have patience, *débarqué*. He took some time to light a cigarette. The effort failed several times. I gave him a helping hand. The flame leapt forth from the lighter that I handed back to him.

He analyzed his mathematical problem.

"Suppose that I have two checkbooks, which happens to be the case at this exact moment, and that each checkbook holds twenty-five checks; in total, then, we have fifty checks, right?"

A little lost, I mumbled, "I think so."

"There's nothing to think about, Marcel, it's completely stupid, it's mathematical!" Fifty checks are more than enough to work with today."

"I still don't see what it is I'm going to do and how we . . ."

He cut me off, on the verge of being irritated, saying, "Stop your blah blah blah. That's normal, you're a rookie. You have to understand things before they are explained to you. In this line of work, there is just one secret: anticipation. The more you anticipate, the more you win."

He came closer to me to speak directly in my ear. I drew back, repulsed by the alcohol on his breath.

"Listen up, *débarqué*, have you ever anticipated anything in your life? Otherwise, open your ears. Line number 4 goes from Porte d'Orléans to Porte de Clignancourt and includes twenty-six subway stations. OK? It's simple. We have to cancel out one to have the exact number of a checkbook: twenty-five. If we make one round-trip, the sum will be correct: fifty stops, fifty checks. That's phase one. We will have used up the checkbooks, but the work won't be over yet. There's still phase two, which is close to my heart. Come with me . . .

—〰—

We arrived at the Porte d'Orléans Métro stop. Préfet made me wait. He wanted to smoke another cigarette. He refused my help with the lighter. He walked away. I kept my eyes on him. I could see him playing a dirty trick on me in an instant. Was he pretending to smoke that cigarette to distract me and achieve his objective?

No. He was talking to himself.

A monologue. A sort of meditation. I drew closer to listen. He stopped me and ordered me not to come closer. When he had finished his cigarette, he crushed the butt under his Weston and came back toward me, his eyes blazing and completely rolled back.

"Listen to me again, *débarqué*. Today is your baptism, so perform good clean work for me. I'm counting on you. The work we are going to accomplish is simple. It's about buying a maximum number of orange coupons, those monthly transit passes, which we will resell on the black market at Château-Rouge tonight for a good price. Do you get the picture?"

He took me by the shoulder. We went separate ways at the Métro entrance. Riders entered and exited the station.

"Hold this."

He handed me a large, slightly crumpled beige envelope. Opening it, I remained speechless. Another identity card, with my photo, identical to the one that I had pulled off the wall of our room. It was a little blurry. But it was me. I could be identified without difficulty. When had he taken this from my stuff? Moki must have been behind this, too. No question. I had a different name than Marcel Bonaventure on the identity card—my name was Eric Jocelyn-George. I couldn't make heads or tails of this anymore. This new ID was manifestly false. Préfet hadn't gone to city hall or to the police station. He had made the ID in a studio, with his own hands.

Scrutinizing the checks, I saw they were in the name of this Eric Jocelyn-George. In other words, me.

I pieced together the network in my mind. Soté the workhorse must have brought back these checkbooks in the name of Eric Jocelyn-George from the provinces. To make the means of payment operational, an identity card was necessary. That was not Soté's specialty. Préfet was brought into the action. Give one of our people the identity of this unknown person. Make an ID in his name. Préfet and Moki had talked about it. I was the latest *débarqué*. The most naïve. My status found favor with Préfet, the great mentor. Moki gave him one of my photos. Préfet worked an entire night to make the fake ID. Everything was perfect: authentic checkbooks, a fake ID, but in the same name as the check holder.

"This is what you are going to work with," he explained, pulling me out of my walking daydream. "You are Eric Jocelyn-George. You go to the window and present *your* identity card with a check. You ask for five coupons for five zones, which must come to more than 2,450 Francs in all. And we repeat the operation at every station until the twenty-sixth, Porte de Clignancourt. Now multiply that amount by the number of stations and we'll have an idea of what we'll have in our pockets by tonight . . ."

I wasn't good in arithmetic. The sum seemed astronomical to me for one day's work: more than 50,000 Francs and close to 60,000. He did the exchange rate for me of the amount in the currency of my country, the Central African Franc: more than five to six million. I remained skeptical.

It was the truth.

Once we were already inside the Porte d'Orléans station, Préfet held me back.

"Final recommendation: Stay calm. Be cool. If the window clerk is fastidious and asks you why five coupons, you blow him off, jabbering about how us blacks have the right to have large families because of the losses we suffered during slavery and all the other stupidities throughout history. And don't forget, we don't know each other. We're in business. It's necessary to take risks. Before buying your coupons, let everyone go in front of you. If the window clerk goes to the telephone, get out of there fast, no hesitating. He could be calling the police . . .

"I think I've told you everything. We can get going. I'll wait for you on the platform while you buy the coupons. We'll start at the next station. Alésia . . ."

A colored woman was the ticket window clerk at Alésia station at the end of that month. I felt at ease, figuring that skin pigment solidarity was a trump card going back to the dawn of time. A man lost in a multiplicity of other humans is on the lookout for someone that looks like him. The gregarious instinct sleeps within us and wakes with a start to dictate this preference, this irrational inclination, which if not quashed, suddenly transforms itself into a blind and irredeemable racism.

I smiled at the woman.

She was on the phone. She put the receiver down, exploding from an inner joy that made me think the person on the other end of the line had touched her G spot with nothing but the magic of verbs. She took her time before returning my completely moronic, inopportune, and circumstantial smile.

She was svelte, very thin, and must have thought her poise to be the eighth wonder of the world. The verdigris uniform and the fine cloth scarf around her neck suited her so well that one could hardly imagine her anywhere except behind this window, next to some maps of Paris, rolls of tickets, a credit card reader, two Harlequin romance novels, and that old telephone that she jumped to answer on the first ring, knocking down everything in the way.

Her youth and clumsiness when she tore off the tickets convinced me she was fresh out of a training program, and she applied her instructions to the letter. I noticed her colleague who appeared in the background. A blond with a ruddy face and a cigarette butt stuck in the hairs of his mustache. He turned around and disappeared behind the service door that opened directly onto the platform where Préfet was waiting for me.

An older woman jabbed me violently in the back with her elbow. I let her go in front of me. She looked me over from head to foot and focused on writing a check with a shaking hand.

I straightened the knot of my tie and cleared my throat. I cast a furtive eye toward the platform. I didn't see Préfet. A short man, he was drowning in the sea of riders. He was supposed to have me under surveillance. He saw me from where he was.

"It's your turn, monsieur," cooed the window clerk through the speaking grill.

"Uhm . . . yes, five . . . five . . . five-zone coupons . . ."

I bit my tongue. What I had said rang false. That's what I thought. All of a sudden, I was scared stiff. The impetus to flee. Why should I flee? Intuition. Inclination. These are things you sense.

I heard a voice behind me.

Another woman of rather advanced age was getting impatient and waved her priority card like a fan. I wanted to let her go ahead.

"You said five coupons?" the window clerk asked.

"Five, for five zones . . ."

Silence.

She used a calculator with her thin fingers and stated a total that was close to 2,400 Francs. I contained my astonishment. I tore off a check. She told me not to fill it out.

So much the better for me—I suddenly remembered that Préfet hadn't taught me how to fill out a check. This form of payment practically didn't exist back home. Only a few functionaries brandished them in front of the rest of the population, who were envious but more loyal to the coin of the realm. To such a degree that, back there, a check was an external sign of wealth, a gauge of permanent solvency. Yet a bank account, in some people's minds, remained an abstract invention by the state and certain shady merchants, their servants, to chisel the savings of the masses of poor people. Why entrust the management of your piggybank to an institution you didn't know much about? And then the rumor went around that the state paid its own debts with the people's money, and it would take centuries and centuries before the state would pay up its bills. It wasn't understood how a country could be in debt. The conclusion drawn was that the president and his ministers paid for their parking garage and the cost of their lifestyle. Under these conditions, as a precautionary measure, back home, money was kept under the mattress in a corner of the house where children were not allowed and where the ancestors we fetishized kept watch night and day and would mercilessly strike every thief with an incurable illness . . .

I couldn't fill out a check, never having seen it done. Another hypothesis came to mind: Préfet had thought it pointless to explain this to me, knowing that checks were filled out only by machines now at these windows.

The station lady scrutinized my identity card in the name of Eric Jocelyn-George. I watched the telephone.

She turned her back to the phone.

A wave of calm passed over me. I breathed. I exhaled so loudly that it visibly bothered the window clerk. She got up with my identity card and checkbook and headed into the other room, closing the door behind her.

My anxiety came racing back.

To flee or not to flee? My stomach was tied in knots. I wanted to go to the toilet. Cold sweat trickled from my armpits and ran down my ribs. I was suffocating in this winter jacket, and I unknotted my tie. The overcoat I carried under my arm became heavy to hold.

Turning around, I saw a long, winding line of customers. I wanted to get out of there now.

My strength abandoned me. I moved my right foot; the left no longer moved on my command. It was time for me to get away from there. And what if there were another telephone inside? Was she in the middle of asking for authorization from the bank or making a call to the police?

To flee.

Push my way through this crowd.

Take the steps two at a time and get out of this station.

No, absolutely don't go out the exit.

The police could only come from the outside. So jump the turnstiles and get on the platform in the hope that a train would arrive that very instant.

And if the woman held up the train?

Too bad, I would have to make a run for it.

My foot finally responded to my multiple requests. A train approached the platform. I heard steps. A race. Riders going down the stairs, going out. Others who were climbing up the stairs. It was time to infiltrate myself into the crowd . . .

I was already near the turnstile when the window clerk rapped on the glass to call me back. Her blond colleague had reappeared. He took note of me without a smile and rubbed his wispy mustache with the back of his hand. He held my identification out in front of his nose and compared me to the photograph on the ID. He nodded his head that it was me, and the window clerk slipped the coupons under the glass after I had signed the check . . .

—ᴡᴡ—

I met up with Préfet on the platform.

He fired away at me with questions. I had dawdled too long. He lost his temper, threatened not to pay me, and refused to listen when I tried to explain how things had unfolded. There was nothing for him to hear, he yelled. He grabbed his coupons out of my hands and stuffed them in his jacket.

He barked:

"Next station: Mouton-Duvernet, and it better go more quickly than this one! . . ."

Could I see this all the way through?

Deep down, I doubted it. There were twenty-four stations left. Twenty-four moments of anguish. I didn't have the right to back out anymore. Forward. Station after station. The whole thing was to keep a cool head and to work energetically. If Préfet was far from satisfied with my work, me, I figured that I had gone to the absolute limits of my capacity . . .

—ᴡᴡ—

It was almost three o'clock in the afternoon.

We had arrived at Château-Rouge and were going to stay there until the black market opened. We had unloaded the twenty-five orange coupons . . .

Before then, things had improved.

The twenty-four stations followed one after the other in my memory. I was stunned by how smoothly things went despite the fright I had experienced.

Even in my dreams, I didn't convince myself that it had been me, Massala-Massala, alias Marcel Bonaventure, alias Eric Jocelyn-George, who was capable of seeing the job through from start to finish. Of course, the eye of the master lurked somewhere in the shadows. An eye that I sensed was behind me. That eye with the sanguine gaze was there. It was on the lookout for the slightest weakness.

Préfet was there, at a distance.

If his presence in the area revolted me, it also reassured me. Revolt because I was the only one working. Reassurance because I felt some sort of protection, almost the benediction of someone who had an entire past history of this type of activity behind him. His experience would be beneficial to me. In the end, I had pulled the chestnuts out of the fire.

From one station to the next, the operation was nothing more than a game. Around eleven o'clock, we took a break. The anxiety, although more tempered than it was when we started, had burned a hole in my stomach. We ate Greek gyros at the Etienne-Marcel Métro stop. I ate enough for two because Préfet, who wasn't hungry, had opened several bottles of Kronenbourg in rapid succession and emptied them like tap water. He belched loudly and had fun rolling his eyes around. He told me that he had no appetite for food until the money was in his pockets.

Wandering around Les Halles, we sat down on a public bench near the boulevard Sébastopol. Then Préfet decided that I had to get back to work, because it was getting close to market time. By that point, we had already *purchased* more than a third of the coupons we needed. That was nothing. An incomplete job, amateur, Préfet hastened to make clear, having sensed my premature satisfaction.

We had to get back to work as soon as possible.

For a moment, I thought I was over the fear, but it came back again after that break we took on boulevard Sébastopol.

It was as if I were back at the first station, in front of the colored woman and her blond colleague. But my reflexes came back. From then on I took the risk of making small talk with the ticket window clerks.

We had gone to the end of the line, Porte de Clignancourt. From there, we made a second trip in the other direction, all the way to Porte d'Orléans, where we had started that morning. The last check was torn out at that station. We had to go back one more time toward Porte de Clignancourt, in the north of Paris, to get to the black market. We got out at Château-Rouge, the marketplace. What remained to be done at that point was to sell the transportation tickets we had *purchased* throughout that heart-stopping day. That didn't faze me. There wouldn't be that whole chaotic circuit we had run from the south to north of Paris and vice versa . . .

—∞—

It was only three o'clock in the afternoon.

According to Préfet, the black market didn't open until around five o'clock in the afternoon. So we sat down in a café. We waited for the right time. Préfet had another beer. He deigned to congratulate me, but half-heartedly. Still not there yet, he added. I had to rise to the challenge, I wasn't quick, my gestures weren't convincing. What was essential had been accomplished; next time, I would have to pull myself together better.

We had to move on to the next phase. The most important, the bit that was close to his heart, in his own words. We were going to reap what we had sown.

Once again, he got straight to the point. I would pull the chestnuts out of the fire. He wasn't going to get involved at this stage, which he was making me do for my own good.

"You have to see your mission through all the way to the end for your baptism to be real. I've always maintained great discretion in this milieu. Nobody must know that I'm here. Get it? It's a question of prudence . . ."

He explained how the second phase would play out. It was in my interest to sell all of the one hundred and twenty-five transit passes that night; otherwise, we would have a hard time finding clients the next day, since another month had begun and everyone, theoretically, had bought their coupon in a station. Primordial rule: absolute discretion. Don't sell to Whites. Get a sense of the client. Watch him come. As soon as he seems suspicious, I shouldn't have any dialogue with him. The client insists? Play dumb:

"'I don't know anything. I don't know what you're talking about. What passes? Ah ha, those are sold here? Whereabouts?' That's how you'll answer suspicious types. Me, I'll be in a corner, near that butcher shop in the marketplace. If a colored customer wants to buy, he'll know how to show it. He's used to it. He'll nod his head several times as if he's in agreement, and you, you'll make the same gesture and indicate with your chin where he should follow you. You'll meet each other at the end of the street. The client will have his cash ready, and the whole thing will take place in a fraction of a second, without saying a word. You have to come back to the café where I am to bring the money from sales as it comes in. To keep a lot of money on you brings bad luck because the others carrying out the same thing get jealous. If, by chance, a police van turns up at the market, stay calm, go into the pharmacy across the street, and wait for them to leave. You mustn't panic. It's an everyday occurrence here. These police sweeps are completely routine. You must know that since you do your shopping here . . ."

I had listened to him talk at length.

He repeated himself, doubted my capacity to sell the transit passes. He was on his umpteenth glass of beer.

The hour passed.

Château-Rouge was full of people. The food market was open until six o'clock. Groups of people were standing around here and there for no apparent reason. The place was abuzz with noise. Comings and goings. Shoving. Mopeds without exhaust pipes. Dilapidated cars that illegally entered the pedestrian lane. Drivers who abandoned their cars on the road.

Another parallel market, the black market, established itself little by little and blended in with the normal market.

First, street peddlers with their cumbersome bags on their backs, leather belts rolled up in spirals in their hands, which they offered to all passersby.

Watch salesmen, with their pants pockets weighed down like a donkey's paunch. One hand quickly burrowed inside and pulled out, in a flash, the appropriate watch for the waiting customer. Other watches hung inside a jacket. The salesmen needed only to undo the buttons of their outfits to offer stunned customers a walking market stall, which made the shopkeepers jealous, those with ironclad faith in licenses and fiscal declarations of commercial and industrial profits.

As for the vendors of cameras and radio cassettes, they sprang up cautiously in the side streets. The weight of their wares dissuaded them from carrying them around on their bodies. Above all, it was the fear of a massive police raid that made them skittish. The police would confiscate their merchandise, the presumed owners having no receipt that could legitimize their claim to ownership. They'd give their eyeteeth to have that. Instead, the vendors rented rooms in the nearby hotel. When a buyer turned up, they showed him photos of their equipment. The buyer then followed them to the hotel where they could try out the equipment in total peace of mind.

—⚉—

"You can go now," Préfet said to me, emptying his last glass of beer.

He left the café to head further down the street to a spot near an intersection where I would come wrap up my sales with customers. From there, he wouldn't miss a single one of my transactions. He took a seat in a different café, the one that I could see from where I stood, one with a large terrace and chairs all the way out to the street.

I got up, too.

The anxiety that I had buried for a good long time came back. As if I were starting the same work over again. As if I were going to turn up in front of every window in the Métro

stations, tear off a check, present the identity card in the name
of that man I didn't know, Eric Jocelyn-George, wait, sign,
take five coupons, find Préfet on the platform, get on the
Métro again to repeat it once more at the next station . . .

I put a hand on my chest to feel my heart beating. Instead,
I felt something that bothered me in the inside pocket of
my jacket. Instinctively, I slipped my hand in to retrieve the
contents . . .

My first photo in Paris.

Those big eyes of an enchanted child. The broken mirror.
The wool blankets. The skylight in our room. The rancid odor.
The clump of earth from my grandmother's grave, there, in
the outside pocket of my overcoat.

I was dreaming on my feet.

I had to get out of this café to wrap up this crazy day. I
couldn't take another step forward. In fact, I didn't want to
go ahead. Préfet was in front of me and challenged me with
his eyes. I stayed put, like marble, jaws clenched in sudden
exasperation. A revolt at the ultimate hour. Like an obstinate
horse that abruptly tries to throw its rider. Préfet was facing
me. I dared to look him in the eye, those eyes that rolled
like white globes amid an invasion of hordes of unidentified
microbes. I held my ground. I wanted to tell him everything
that I thought about this affair. I wanted to capitulate. Lower
my arms. Throw down my weapons. I was sick of it. Then a
sentence took shape suddenly from the bottom of my throat:

"Let's get serious. How much is my cut going to be from
this?"

Préfet, who wasn't expecting this, replied icily: "Around
here, we never sell the bear skin before killing the bear."

"I don't give a damn about that. I'm not moving if I don't
know how much will be turned over to me. I am ready to
settle for 20,000 Francs for . . ."

"Let's say, 15,000 . . ."

"I said 20,000."

"You forget that you owe me for the cost of your identity
papers. You forget that I've got to pay the workhorse, who

gave me the checkbooks. You forget that I have to pay Moki, who provided me with what I might call a hired hand. You forget that your work uniform, I bought it with my own money, that's a Cerruti you've got there, my man, I don't know if you were aware of that. And you forget all this? Like all the *débarqués*, you're nothing but an ingrate. We can't sell these passes for the same price they're sold at the windows. On the black market, we lower the prices, otherwise, what's the point of it? We'll have more or less 45,000 Francs, and you want to claim 20,000!"

"I find that an equitable division."

"Twenty thousand Francs, that's the price of an identity paper; I wouldn't have to give you anything if I held you to that. Once again, I'm indulgent. I reiterate my offer for you to take it or leave it. Think it over carefully: 15,000 Francs, and you won't owe me anything more . . ."

Silence.

"Get going. Don't lose any more time. Get to work!"

I remained standing, next to the butcher shop.

He left to take a seat on the terrace at the café down the street. From a distance, I saw him change seats. He gestured to me with his head.

A moment's hesitation.

I made my decision.

I wanted to get this business over with as quickly as possible so that I could breathe. A mental calculation made me understand that with 15,000 French Francs, in my country, I would be affluent, with a million and a half Central African Francs. I would be a millionaire.

I would be satisfied with this amount. As happy as I would be to never owe anything else to Préfet.

I took the first step.

I left the café to move toward the customers . . .

I had sold a few transit passes to more than a dozen customers, for the most part Blacks and North Africans, sometimes
even some Hindus, whose exuberant smiles made clear to me
that they were part of this imbroglio.

I was amused to see how customers approached me without ignorant passersby suspecting a thing. They nodded their
heads quickly. I replied and indicated with the same gestures
to follow me to the end of the street. I walked in front. We
took a narrow, winding side street that reeked of urine. The
transaction took place there, in complete clandestinity, the
street being nearly deserted. I haven't forgotten the pigeons. In
fact, we weren't the only ones who appreciated discreet loca-
tions. In addition to the women who ran there, hiked up their
skirts to their butts, and spread their legs to urinate, we visibly
disturbed other creatures: pigeons who fled our approach and
perched, quarrelsome and angry, on the decrepit buildings'
rooftops. They complained loudly in their language and came
back the moment we turned around.

Transaction accomplished, I went back down the street, this
time with my customers in the lead. Before returning to the
spot where I met my customers, I branched off to the right to
deposit the take where Préfet was waiting for me, beady business eyes on of a glass of beer overflowing with foam.

I had adopted an optimistic framework: in less than an
hour, I could get rid of the remaining passes.

The demand far exceeded the supply . . .

I waited for customers.

Night would catch hold of us in not much time. The market
slowed down. So did my optimism. I had exaggerated a bit. But
it was necessary to wait. Préfet had said: some customers quit
work around six o'clock in the evening. They come from all
over, even from the most faraway suburbs in the Île-de-France
region. By the time they get to the market, night would surely
fall upon them. Meanwhile, these coupons never went back
with him. They were going to be sold, no matter what. In the
worst case, we would have to adjust our price—after all, what
use were these passes once the month had passed or was well
underway?

—∭—

I had less than twenty transit passes left. Weary of standing on the street, my feet numb, I moved across the street to lean against a wall less fouled by urine.

I crossed the street.

Little by little, the marketplace emptied out. Market vendors consulted each other, establishing obscure accounts, exchanging merchandise with each other. The customers weren't biting anymore. You had to take them by the hand, insist, convince them, negotiate the price. I didn't have it in me to put up with skinflints at this point. Just by the way I was standing, they could sense that I was the one who sold coupons. A little like that very dark-skinned man, tall, who twisted his neck to show by impetuously nodding his head that he wanted a transit pass.

I responded to him and indicated with my chin which way to go.

He smiled at me.

White teeth. Thick lips. A large mouth that led me to conclude, without other evidence, that he had more teeth than a normal man and his laugh, the least you could say about it was it belonged to a halfwit.

I went down the main street; the man followed me without hesitation. He kept on making approving gestures with his head.

I was at his service.

The pigeons flew away from the street.

They went back to screeching from the rooftops. A little further down, I noticed Préfet's shadow on the terrace.

Nobody.

A man in a white apron swept the entrance to the café and lined the chairs up, one on top of another.

Well? Where did he go?

Taking the right fork, I realized that something had just happened in that side street. I should have walked as if I were going to visit someone in one of the surrounding buildings. I lifted my head instinctively: two men were coming toward me at a quick pace. A little further, a badly parked car took up the entire street.

A white Mazda.

It wasn't there before. I remember clearly. It hadn't been there. I tried to turn back the other way. The Black with the idiotic smile who nailed me just to buy transit passes ordered me, stone faced, to keep on going to the car. He dangled a set of handcuffs in the air and, taking long strides, caught up with me, while the other two men, one tall and one short, pinned me to the car and frisked me roughly. No resistance on my part. My feet stayed on the ground. My body weighed heavy, burning up inside while my heart beat violently against my chest.

The pigeons ogled us from above . . .

The two men seized my fake IDs, the checkbook stubs, the unsold transit passes, and my first photo in Paris. The short man, more aggressive than the tall one, took away my overcoat shook it out, and removed the clump of earth from my grandmother's grave from my pocket. He unwrapped it and sniffed. I heard him ask himself, skeptically, "What kind of new drug is this?"

I hear some noise behind the door.

Someone is trying to open it. Practically break it down. He delivers a few kicks, turns the key in the locks, and mutters a stream of abuse.

The same people as yesterday, no doubt. The ones who brought me here. The tall one and the short one.

There they are. They've come back. I wonder what the meaning is of these comings and goings. With every commotion outside, I tell myself that perhaps the time has come. And then they leave again, without telling me a damn thing.

Here they are . . .

The light is going to daze me.

The light? I don't know what time it is. I've slept a lot, and I can't figure out when I fell asleep. Is it a dream that has plunged me back into the past? Before closing my eyes, there were pictures. Moki. Préfet. Moki again. Préfet again.

I can't remember anything anymore.

I must make the effort to remember. Just as I had done up to now. I'm not dreaming. Things are going to happen fast. My situation surely depends on that door, which is opening.

What happened?

I'm going to remember. The white Mazda that cut off the whole side street. I've got nothing more than a shadow of the man who threw me in this room. The short man. The more aggressive of the two. His muscular hands on my shoulders. They slammed the door shut with a big bang. Then they left precipitously without telling me what was going to happen next.

Now they're here. Behind the door.

I must remember.

The car, parked badly, on the street. The two men walking toward each other. I didn't run. I put up no resistance. Was that my mistake? Then they pinned me down. The Black was one of them. He was working with them. He had pretended that he wanted to buy transit passes. Who gave the game away? How did they know our gang's signals?

In the Mazda, it was the Black guy who drove.

They had put me in handcuffs. I was in the back, flanked by the two other men, circumspect and sinister. They seemed to breathe in unison. They looked straight ahead. The taller one said to the driver:

"Head toward the fourteenth arrondissement, rue du Moulin-Vert . . ."

—〰—

On rue du Moulin-Vert, the two men lifted me like a suitcase to climb the stairs of our building. The Black guy, violent, knocked down the door to the room with a blow from his shoulder and nearly fell on the wool blankets. Nobody was in the room. They were annoyed, pissed off, and made me sit on the floor. The shorter one barked, "Where's Préfet?"

His eyes were on fire. His muscular body looked like it was waiting for the right moment to deliver a fatal blow to my face.

"I don't know anything," I said, protecting my face.

The short man got annoyed and fumbled inside his jacket, pulled out an envelope and tore it open clumsily.

"And this? What's this?" he yelled at the top of his voice.

He tossed two black-and-white Polaroid photos at my legs. In the first one, Préfet and I were talking in front of the Porte d'Orléans Métro station. He had a cigarette between his lips. I listened to him, attentively, just like a disciple drinking up the words of his master with blind devotion. In the second one, we were in a café at Château-Rouge. He had taken the transit passes out of a pocket of his jacket. He prepared to count them before giving them back to me. I wasn't in a good mood. This was after the argument that we had had about how much I would make.

"So you still don't know where your accomplice crashes?" the short man said sarcastically while I looked guilty and confused.

The specter of Préfet was there.

He had woven a web of mystery about where he lived. That was his strength. I knew that. He didn't live anywhere. Who among us could say where he slept? Préfet did not have an ordinary existence. He was equipped for that. To escape from the police. He imposed a severe discipline on himself. A complicated schedule. Many of us would refuse a life like that. He didn't take the same route. His movements were never habitual. Didn't see the same people. Didn't give them the opportunity to set up meetings. Didn't tell them when he was coming over. Arrived at their house unexpectedly. Never had his picture taken with the other Parisians. Avoided public places like Les Halles, the Champs-Elysées, and the Gare du Nord. At Château-Rouge, he stayed in the background, the grand orchestrator of operations. All his precautions made him claustrophobic. He didn't like to come into our room. For him it was a dangerous trap. Every footstep on the floor made him nervous. He waited on the ground floor and predicted that one day we would be caught like dragonflies.

A shadow darkened my thoughts: since we had been photographed with Préfet, why did they allow him to disappear instead of finally arresting him?

The reply seemed blatantly obvious to me. They wanted to track the network back to its ringleaders. Learn how we operated. How many of us were there? Who was high up? Where besides Château-Rouge were we selling these transit passes? The police were not very satisfied with bribes. When they leave you time to breathe, it's only to set the big trap. Don't spread your wings in joy. Don't ring the victory bell too soon. Somewhere, in putting it back together, an element of the puzzle doesn't fit or was put in the wrong place. Then the police take their time to look into it, to remove it, to scrutinize it, to compare it with others, to put it back when the right place is established. That could take days, weeks, and more often than not, entire years. In our milieu, we joked that the French police were the slowest in the world but the most efficient. A praying mantis, not a fly agitated by the smell of defecation . . .

Préfet sensed the suspicious atmosphere in the street and must have deflected the attention of these men. They would have let us keep on going until we were finished and then would have swept us up, just as Préfet had thought. They would go to where he lived and discover the materials for forgery and other compromising documents.

That's it: Préfet, having disappeared, left me alone, the only one in a position to tell them where he lived.

"For the last time, where does Préfet live?"

"I have no idea."

They turned the room inside out, threw the blankets out the window, tore the bits of wallpaper remaining on the cracked walls, turned over the plastic table, and opened the skylight to look on the roof.

In frustration, the taller one shook his finger at me and yelled, "All right, get this one out of here!"

While the black guy twisted my arms, the short man seized the opportunity he'd been waiting for to kick me in the butt.

Several weeks had already passed since I'd found myself in the darkness of the Seine-Saint-Denis jail for the first time. I was alone, cloistered, in a cell in the A wing, B building, fourth floor. I had a view of the courtyard and a few nearby rooftops. I climbed onto the bed and gripped the iron bars of that little window. I saw guards making their rounds with bulldogs and prisoners from the facing building exercising and playing volleyball. Police vehicles came and went all day long with their captives.

Within the four walls of the prison. I didn't want to think about all the people from our world. I wanted to create a void around me. Not think of anything but myself, about nobody else.

To listen to the internal voices of my conscience was a harsh test. I swept away with the back of my hand the thoughts that inflicted me with remorse. I didn't succeed, despite that. I faced a mirror. The man I found there intimidated me. I couldn't pull myself away. His big eyes stared at me without blinking. His stricken face pitied me. His drawn features emphasized that these events had exhausted him. I held out my hand to touch him. I noticed that I held out a hand to myself. I was far gone. I had been in a hole since the verdict fell on me like a cleaver.

—∞—

Nobody came to see me at the jail. And for good reason: the visitor would have met the same fate as me. I didn't receive any letters either. That was one of the rules in our circle. We didn't know each other anymore. I had become dirty. I had failed in my mission. I was not worthy of the milieu.

Where had Préfet gone? Where had Moki gone? Had they sent news of my incarceration back home? I was sure that they hadn't. It was in their interest to lie for the sake of keeping up appearances.

The face my father would make!

His wise words. Don't listen to anything but the voice of your conscience: *"Be careful, keep your eyes open, and don't act until your conscience—not someone else's—guides you. These will be my final words, I, your father, who has nothing and envies nothing belonging to anyone . . ."*

I had stayed locked up in that interminable night. I didn't know what light or liberty meant anymore. I could only invent light with the gleam of memories. I hooked myself on a thread of hope. One day, the light would burst forth, illuminate the horizon. For now, the night reigned.

To live in darkness changes a man.

I knew that when I studied myself one day in the pail filled with water in the center of the courtyard of the jail. I gazed at myself like that. My features fluctuated in the liquid, metamorphosed in the bucket. I discovered a strange man, a man who shocked me. The bony face, the shaggy beard, the hair cropped short by another prisoner.

I was that man.

I imagined the reflection of that face in the broken mirror of our room on Moulin-Vert. I wouldn't recognize myself. I had a different face. Facing charges that kept me on my feet. Charges that immobilized me in this place.

The indictment was a burden that outweighed my moral strength. Condemned for complicity in fraud, identity theft, forgery, and use of forgeries and other sprawling infractions whose juridical terminology made me leap out of the dock, I learned to my great distress that French law was tougher on the accomplices than the main actors. My lawyer, a court-appointed lawyer, replaced himself at the last minute with his trainee, a young person of mixed race, pretentious, who listened to himself talk so much, instead of defending me, that he spent the entire morning reciting his course on special penal code and criminology to the judges who were half asleep.

Outside, they had forgotten me.

I was a man without identity, me who, at one time, had taken on several. I didn't know anymore who I really was. Massala-Massala, my real name? Marcel Bonaventure, my adopted name? Eric Jocelyn-George, my work name?

To forget oneself.

To be nothing more than an anonymous man. Without a past. Without a future. Condemned in the immediate present to carry on day after day, gaze lowered. A man who has lost his way, hounded by remorse, tormented by the night, devoured by exhaustion.

I was another man . . .

I had learned the virtue of silence.

In the darkness, I discovered those shadows, faces, pictures of my homeland, the only loyal loves that exuded a *joie de vivre* in me, the hope of stepping past this cold wall one day. I dreamed, beyond this cell, of a space of happiness, sober and honest.

My homeland was there. Nearby.

My homeland was there. From its breasts flowed that warm milk, rich and nourishing, which I drank greedily. Those breasts that I pressed with all my strength.

My homeland was there.

Around that time, the seeds must have sprouted from the bosom of the earth. The blue sky was spread out against the enormity of the horizon, the brush fires came one after another, and the birds returned from their distant migration.

My homeland was there.

The prison was a walk through the desert, one that put me face to face with my responsibilities. One that showed me that fate was a broken line, a terrain dotted with sand bars that impede the journey.

That was my France.

One of night. The night of thoughts. The night of vagabond-age. The night of walls.

Where was the light? Where had the sun gone?

Part of me hated myself, and the other part exonerated me. I looked for a way out. I looked for redemption. I would have to conquer that, not wait for it like the other prisoners accustomed and resigned to their fate. Not wait for it in blissful fatality. Get out of this place as quickly as possible.

Redemption is a long march. You have to get up early, take provisions, water, and something to cover yourself when night falls. I had to move toward it. Redemption wasn't going to move toward me.

The road to redemption passed through good behavior. It was in my interest to conduct myself irreproachably in order to get the attention of those whose mission it was to set us on a new path.

I also spoke little. I obeyed. I made my prison bed as soon as I got up. I would have loved to read. I didn't have that chance. No book, no paper in the building to scrawl everything that passed through my head. To write letters that didn't arrive at their destination. To report my pain and suffering. To draw the face of freedom. A bird of light with its wings spread.

Read, meditate. Read more and meditate. I invented my daily prayers. With my own words. According to my mood. I didn't ask for anything specific from the supreme being. He who had left me on this precipice. I simply took communion with my own kind back home.

The path to redemption opened up.

I was as courteous to my fellow prisoners as I was to the jail-house personnel. I didn't respond to the escapades of others. God alone knows how many times I was confronted by this. I kept my distance from the confabs and plans for undercover maneuvers that ended up right in the guards' ears. Punishment was swift. Confinement in a humid place, banished, dark, and with the bonus of a reputation as a renegade, which compromised any plan for clemency.

I agreed to learn carpentry during my incarceration. I put on blue overalls. There were many of us who followed a teacher to the penitentiary's workshop. The machines hummed. We were closely supervised. I learned how to work with wood, how to handle a plane, to drill a plank, to build floorboards, to hammer a nail without bending it, to saw with dexterity. A few months later, I put together chairs, tables, bookshelves, and especially benches that we would sit on in the dining hall courtyard. I received a certificate at the end of my apprenticeship. I had a skill now. These hands were good for something. I was still waiting for redemption . . .

The hunger strike called by the rowdy convicts was none of my business. They must have hated me. Me, I ate. I emptied my bowl with a healthy appetite and finished my bread down to the last crumb. The hunger strike didn't concern me. I wasn't here to agitate, to change the establishment's penal policies. Why fight to change the conditions of a milieu that I had to get out of, at all cost? If militancy existed, I would have liked to see evidence of it for the purpose of digging the fastest way to freedom. Not liberty acquired under the cover of evasion, something I found abominable—I had to pay, no matter what, and I took that on—but in my soul and conscience, it was merited.

That freedom, could I attain it?

That was another story. First it was necessary to get out of the jailhouse . . .

CLOSING

THE LIGHT DAZZLED MY EYES.

The door is open.

The two silhouettes are in front of me. One tall and one short. A voice asks me to get up and to go into the next room to wash up.

"The charter leaves in exactly three hours, get a move on!"

The charter.

They're going to carry out the judge's decision.

I want to go past rue du Moulin-Vert one last time. "*Out of the question,*" they said. They are strict. "*You have no business there anymore, we've sealed the room, and we're looking for your friend and his followers.*"

I learn that we'll make stops in several African capitals: Bamako, Dakar, Kinshasa, and finally Brazzaville. In this last city, which is in my country, I will be left to my own fate, they say, but with a few French Franc notes in my pocket. I don't know Brazzaville. From there, I'll take the train, then an all-terrain vehicle will take me all the way to my neighborhood, several kilometers outside Congo's coastal city, Pointe-Noire.

The prospect of going back rattles me.

I'm nothing more than a good for nothing. I'm nothing but a wreck. A failure. I hadn't prepared myself for that. Couldn't they give me a few months, the time to put together a little suitcase of clothes, some presents for the family? I was so naïve I thought these two men might help me. Silence. I have to leave France. I'm a black sheep. A dead branch . . .

In the shower, the thought of suicide takes hold of me. The thought matures as the departure time nears. The tap is open, water is escaping everywhere, all the way to the door. I don't turn off the faucet. The water is still running. It's too hot. It's still running. I'm not stopping it. The room is flooded. Like a sauna. I can't see anything in front of my nose anymore. Only the noise of water. Drops of water. A flood. A diluvian rainfall. Mist. Burning skin. I suppress the pain. Crush my carotid artery. Crack my skull against the sink. Plug my nostrils. A few minutes would be all it would take. Just a few minutes. Without a single cry.

I glorify that act.

Why hadn't I thought of it before?

To kill oneself, what could be more heroic? To not entrust one's fate to the line drawn by a creator, whoever that may be. Facing the wall, a man can decide: withdraw or confront it. Confrontation? Withdrawal?

—∞—

Somebody knocks on the door to the shower.

"You've got no more than five minutes!"

My heart jumps and sinks in my stomach. I have a stomachache. Down to my pubic bone. Boils everywhere. On the skin. The hot water burned me. I'm contorted with pain. I feel something else now burning the length of my thighs. A hot liquid. Not as hot as the water from the tap. But hot. I can't hold my urine anymore. I want to defecate.

I can't hold it.

Nude, I look at those shrunken genitals, those contracted balls. The excrement floats in water by my feet. I am not a man anymore.

I know what's in store for me. I didn't have the courage to stop breathing. To let myself burn. To split my skull. To crush my carotid artery. I chose to confront another reality. I chose to see this through to the end.

I would go home.

I would be the laughingstock of the neighborhood. But I would be home. There, I would turn an indifferent ear to the

crowd pointing a finger at me. People will say whatever they
want. They will tell me off, be revolted by me. They'll give it
a rest someday. I'm not afraid of these prosecutors anymore.
They don't take the time to understand everything. They don't
know that the world we live in is a different world. In a milieu
that we barely see, nothing can be foreseen. Nothing at all.
We don't foresee. We suffer. We allow ourselves to be carried by the current. We are taught elementary reflexes, current expressions. We are told how to look, what to eat, how
to drink. You are nothing but chum surrounded by sharks.
There's nothing you can do but follow the beat. And in that
world over there, the beat is normally frenzied. If you walk
along slowly, worn out by endless repetition, a whipping will
remind you that here, slowness is prohibited.

   We are caught in a circle. We are serpents biting our own
tails. Our circle is there. Without a spoke. Without that fixed
central point. So we gravitate to the inside. Our circle is a sort
of trap with no way out. Each of us has his own story. In the
end, they all intersect. And we come back to Moki's expression: *Paris is a big boy* . . .

   I will go home.

   I don't fear what's in store for me anymore. I don't care
about anything except my old mother, a silent woman,
resigned and virtuous, who will surely be overwrought by the
news of my inopportune return. She will not tolerate her son
being the laughingstock of the neighborhood. The women in
the marketplace will not make her life easy.

   I grieve equally for my father, a proud man who had placed
his hope in me. His words haunt me. I didn't apply them.
There was nothing I could do about it. I grieve for him. He
made a fool of himself, bowing down before my uncle to ask
for money to pay for my ticket. Would he know that these
two years were blank and that I had rotted in total darkness
at the expense of the French government? I'll tell him that.
From him, I will hide nothing. I'll invite him to come behind
our house. We'll speak man to man. I'll tell him everything,
from beginning to end. I'll give my uncle the little bit of money
they had given me to wander around Brazzaville. No. I'll give

it all to my father instead. He could take care of reimbursing
my uncle.

And my sister? And Adeline? And my son? My sister would
readily understand me. She would laugh, with tears in her
eyes. We were born to live side by side. Like twins. She would
speak to my mother about it. They would cry a little. Especially
the first few days. Would Adeline stay at the house? She will
leave. With or without the child. I can't predict it. I know her
a little. She will leave. I would be one of those back home they
call the *Parisian rejects.*

And then it would all pass.

A new sky would appear. A new season would begin.
The rainy season. The downpours would bring landslides of
dreams still embedded on the slopes of memory. Only time
can erase the vestiges of a deflected existence. We would stay,
all four of us, my father, my mother, my sister, and me, in that
hovel. With my son, if Adeline would allow it. We would stay
there. Like in the old days. In that house where we were born.
We would light the place with a hurricane lamp or candle
when we didn't have enough money to buy gas. We would
get water from next door, at Moki's house. My father would
not be brought into the village council. That's life. My mother,
she would pick up her basin of peanuts again and sell at the
big market until the end of her days, like Pindy's mother, who
died at the age of ninety without missing a day of business.
She raised us with what little she had. My father will expect
nothing but his modest pension. One has to live.

For that, we would do everything.

It's not the white car, the Mazda, that's going to take me. It's a police van.

I see faces of other Africans in the courtyard. They are surrounded by uniformed officers, billy clubs in hand. The Africans are resigned. Heartache is written clearly on their faces. They are going back despite themselves. It's not so much the need to stay that torments them but the fear of confronting a whole large family that awaits them. Like me. This difficult reality. This other reality that we can't shake off. Those hands held out toward us. The family that encircles you. That's our fear. It takes guts to come back from a long trip empty-handed, without a present for your mother, for your father, for your brothers and sisters. This anguish resides inside your throat. It stifles your reason for living.

They are there, the others to be expelled. The undesirable. I'm the last one into the courtyard, still escorted by my two men. We're told to line up. They have to count us. Like merchandise.

They count heads. They make a mistake. They start over. They make a mistake again. They start over again. They divide us into small groups. No. By country, finally. That's better. It seems that this is more practical. It's to avoid having those who don't know how to speak and understand French wind up in a country that isn't theirs. Moreover, some come from two countries. Others don't remember their countries anymore. Too bad, their memories will come back on the charter. They all pretend, and when they glimpse a cloud over their homeland, a sudden excitement grabs hold of them.

As for me, there's a problem. A tiny little problem. I have no compatriots among those being expelled. A police officer who had done a tour of duty in French Equatorial Africa whispers to his colleagues that they can put me in the group of Zairians because we speak the same language on both banks of the Congo (or Zaire) River. Both sides speak Lingala. The officer stops, turns around, takes this to be a joke and titters, as if to say to the other one, "Stop treating me like a halfwit." He hadn't done a tour of duty in French Equatorial Africa, he says, but he knows a few things about central Africa, he had read *stuff* about it, and his grandfather had been governor back in the good old colonial times, etc.

The veteran insists and approaches us in Lingala, with a French accent that strips the language of all its elegance:

"M'boté na bino baninga!"[1]

1. Hello my friends!

I doze on the shoulder of my Zairian neighbor.

It's been hours already since France was no longer below us. Night has fallen. The journey will be longer than when I came to France because of the stops in the other African capitals.

I will be going back to the starting box.

I almost laugh about it. In three months, the dry season will batter the country. It's the season of youthful effervescence. The Parisians come home.

Moki will descend with his blue-white-red dream. I wonder whether I'll go out of my way to see him. I would like to hear what he would say to me in the first place.

I think that I'll go and see him anyway.

Maybe he'll convince me to try my luck again?

What would I say to him?

You never can tell.

I can't say how I would answer him. I'm undecided on the subject. Everything is possible in this world of ours. Without being aware of it, I'm no longer the same. I honestly think that I wouldn't tell him no. I prepare myself mentally. I can't rule out the possibility of returning to France. I think I will go back. I can't live with a fiasco on my conscience. It's a matter of honor. Yes, I will go back to France . . .

Did I say go back?

Am I asleep or awake? What difference does it make? There's no border between dreams and reality here anymore.

—ɯɯ—

The plane struggles in the clouds like a heavy bird chased out of the sky by an imminent storm. We all sleep. It's the only moment when we can forget the face-to-face that awaits us with our family members, the immediate family and the most distant who will come running from the villages to demand their piece of the pie . . .

Paris, September 1993,
May 1995

Alain Mabanckou was awarded the Grand Prix Littéraire de l'Afrique Noire for his first novel, *Bleu-Blanc-Rouge*. Since that time, he has published several prize-winning novels. His latest work, *Mémoires de porc-épic* [*Memoirs of a Porcupine*], has won the Prix Renaudot, the Prix Aliénor d'Aquitaine, and the Prix de la rentrée littéraire française. He is considered one of the leading voices of modern French literature. He lives in Los Angeles and has a professorship in the French and Francophone Studies Department at the University of California, Los Angeles. He is an active promoter and gives lectures nationwide. His blog, in French, is considered an essential stop for those monitoring the pulse of Francophone literature.

Alison Dundy lives in New York City and works as a librarian, archivist, and translator. Her translation of Sony Labou Tansi's *Life and a Half* was published by Indiana University Press in 2011.

CPSIA information can be obtained
at www.ICGtesting.com
Printed in the USA
EDOW021415250113
519ED